A
NASTY
PIECE
OF
WORK

ALSO BY ROBERT LITTELL

Fiction

Young Philby
The Stalin Epigram
Vicious Circle
Legends
The Company
Walking Back the Cat
The Visiting Professor
An Agent in Place
The Once and Future Spy
The Revolutionist
The Sisters
The Amateur
The Debriefing
Mother Russia
The October Circle
Sweet Reason
The Defection of A.J. Lewinter

Nonfiction

For the Future of Israel (with Shimon Peres)

A NASTY PIECE OF WORK

Robert Littell

DUCKWORTH OVERLOOK

First published in the UK in 2014 by
Duckworth Overlook
30 Calvin Street, London E1 6NW
T: 020 7490 7300
E: info@duckworth-publishers.co.uk
www.ducknet.co.uk
For bulk and special sales, please contact
sales@duckworth-publishers.co.uk
or write to us at the address above

© 2013 by Robert Littell

First published in the USA by Thomas Dunne Books.

This is a work of fiction. All of the characters, organizations, and
events portrayed in this novel are either products of the
author's imagination or are used fictitiously.

A catalogue record for this book is available
from the British Library

ISBNs
Hardback: 978-0-7156-4734-9
Paperback: 978-0-7156-4821-6

Printed and bound in the UK by
TJ International Ltd, Padstow, Cornwall

Pour Vanessa, ma fille d'escalier

The Principal Characters in This Book

Lemuel Gunn, a New Jersey homicide detective turned CIA agent turned private investigator, working out of an all-aluminum mobile home (used by Douglas Fairbanks Jr. when he was filming *The Prisoner of Zenda*) parked in Hatch, New Mexico. Psychologically speaking, there is a strong possibility Gunn may have been born into the wrong century.

Ornella Neppi, a thirty-something professional puppeteer cum bail bondsman cum barefoot contessa wearing just enough clothing to avoid being arrested for indecent exposure. She turns up at Gunn's mobile home hoping against hope he will help her out of a jam and is relieved when, for ninety-five dollars a day plus expenses, he agrees to give it his best shot.

Emilio Gava, the source of Ornella Neppi's jam, busted for buying cocaine in Las Cruces, New Mexico. He may be jumping the bail she posted to get him out of jail. Curiously, no photographs of him seem to exist.

France-Marie, the divorced French Canadian accountant who keeps Gunn's books but doesn't understand the music men make and won't play second fiddle.

Kubra Ziayee, the Afghan orphan Gunn adopted during his tour in Kabul. She got American citizenship using the name Ziayee but signed up for classes at a California junior college under the name Gunn, which tickled her adopted father to tears.

Charlie Coffin, a balding Caucasian Peeping Tom in his fifties who decided it was time for Muhammad to come to the mountain. He has the street smarts to freeze when a Q-tip is jammed into his ear.

Plus a cast of dozens: assorted police officers, journalists, security guards, concierges, poker players, bartenders, FBI agents, secretaries, and secretaries of secretaries, lawyers, hardware store proprietor and son, hair stylists, casino proctologists, and the neighborhood Nevada mafiosi who employ them.

A
NASTY
PIECE
OF
WORK

One

Some things you get right the first time. With me it was cutting fuses to booby-trap Kalashnikovs being shipped to footloose Islamic warriors looking for a convenient jihad. It was making a brush pass with a cutout in the souk of Peshawar. Other things, no matter how many times you do them, you don't do them better. Which I suppose explains why I still can't make sunny-sides up without breaking the yolk. Which is why I refuse to leave messages at the sound of the beep. Which is why I wear my father's trusty stem-winding Bulova instead of one of those newfangled motion-powered watches. Which is why I put off wrestling with the IRS's 1040 until the divorced French Canadian lady accountant in Las Cruces comes by to hold my hand. My pet hate this week is balancing the monthly statement I get from the Las Cruces Savings and Loan over on Interstate 25. I have this recurrent fantasy that this craze for plastic with built-in credit lines and buy-now, pay-later schemes is this year's skirt length, that consenting adults are bound to wise up and come home to the crisp comfort of cold cash. I once made the mistake of sharing this fantasy with my lady accountant but she only rolled over in my bed and treated me to a short course on how credit greases the economic skids. At which point I trotted out the Will Rogers chestnut I'd come across in the *Albuquerque Times Herald* and squirreled away for just such an occasion, something about how an economist's opinion is likely to be as good as anyone's. What could France-Marie say except "touché." True to form, she managed to pronounce it with a French Canadian accent.

The other thing on my hit list, as long as I'm on the subject, is flushing out septic tanks. If you live in a mobile home, which I do, it's something you have got to deal with eventually. I'd put it off so long there was this distinctly unpleasant sloshing down in the bowels of the Once in a Blue Moon every time someone went to the john. Made it hard to fall asleep, made it harder to stay asleep after you fell asleep when the lady accountant from Las Cruces slept over. So I'd finally gotten around to connecting the hose to the park's sewage line and, using an adjustable wrench I'd borrowed from a neighbor five mobile homes down, started up my spanking-new self-priming pump. When the sump gurgled empty, I closed the line and unhooked it. Crawling out from under my mobile home, I cut across half a dozen yards to return the wrench, then came back by the street side to retrieve Friday's *Albuquerque Times Herald,* along with the fistful of ads stuffed into my mailbox. I was checking out the headline—something about Republican senators defending the construction of a missile shield to protect America from an attack the Russians were unlikely to launch—when I noticed the footprints in the sand. Someone had come down the walkway between the street and my front door. They were light prints set on the surface of the sand path, as if the person responsible for making them was featherweight, with the turned-out profile that suggested a ballet dancer's way of walking. Coming up to the Once in a Blue Moon, I batted away a kamikaze flight of insects and squinted into the brutal New Mexican sun and found myself staring at a very shapely pair of naked ankles.

I saluted the ankles respectfully. "You must be Friday," I said.

The voice attached to the ankles turned out to be a throaty contralto that sounded as if it had surfed through several hours of scales. "Why Friday?" she asked.

I must have shrugged, which is what I usually do when I make a joke that goes over somebody's head. "That's how Robinson Crusoe came across the visitor on his island—he found footprints in the sand on the beach. Called his visitor Friday because of the day of the week this happened. Today's a Friday. Robinson Crusoe? Daniel Defoe? Ring a bell?"

She favored me with the faintest of smiles devoid of any residue of joy. "You can call me Friday if it tickles you. I'm looking for a Mr. Lemuel Gunn."

I was still wearing my septic-pumping finery, a decrepit pair of once-white mechanic's overalls which, to make matters worse, had shrunk in the wash. I shifted my weight from foot to foot a bit more clumsily than I would have liked. I've been told I have good moves when it comes to what in polite

circles is called hand-to-hand combat but women somehow
bring out the elbows in me. I blinked away more of the sunlight and began to make her out. The barefoot contessa was
pushing thirty from the wrong side and tall for a female of
the species, at least five-ten in her deliciously bare feet. Two
rowboat-sized flat-soled sandals dangled from a forefinger; a
bulky silver astronaut-fabric knapsack hung off one gorgeous
shoulder. She had prominent cheekbones, a slight offset to
an otherwise presentable nose, a gap between two front teeth,
faint worry lines around her eyes and mouth. Her eyes were
seaweed green and deep-set and solemn and blinked about
as often as those of the Sphinx. Her lips were straight out of
a Scott Fitzgerald novel, oval and moist and slightly parted
in permanent perplexity. Everything, as Mr. Yul Brynner
used to tell us six nights a week and Saturday matinees, is a
puzzlement. Her hair was short and straight and dark and
tucked back behind her ears. She wasn't wearing makeup,
at least none that I could spot. There wasn't a ring on a finger, a bracelet on a wrist, a necklace on the neck she had
swiped from a swan. Take me as I am, she seemed to be
saying. Minimum packaging, just enough so she wouldn't
be arrested for indecent exposure, though on second glance
she was even pushing the legal limits on that. She was wearing a wispy knee-length skirt with a pleasant flowery print,
and a butter-colored sleeveless blouse that left a sliver of midriff exposed. Both the skirt and blouse seemed to respond to a
current of air, a whisper of wind I couldn't feel on my skin.
This private breeze of hers plastered the skirt against a long
supple thigh, and the blouse against the torso enough to

make out several very spare ribs and the outline of a single nipple.

My luck, it was pointing straight at me.

In my bankrupt state—I'm talking emotions, not savings and loan; my relationship with the lady accountant from Las Cruces was going nowhere fast—she seemed like the proverbial breath of fresh air, stirring a memory of passions past. I'd had two or three unpleasant episodes with women in the fourteen months since my discharge. Once I hadn't been able to finish what I'd started, which was a new and frightening experience for me. Now, for the first time in a long time, I relished the pleasure of imagining the body under the cloth draped over it. For the first time in a long time I felt I'd have no trouble rising to the occasion.

She suffered my once-over in silence, then shook her head impatiently. "So do you or don't you?" she asked. "Answer to the name of Lemuel Gunn?"

I heard myself reach for the glib response and hated myself for it. "Sorry, sweetheart, but I gave at the office."

"No offense intended but you don't look like someone who's ever seen the inside of an office."

The conversation had gotten off on the wrong foot and she knew it. Trying to set it right, she summoned from the depths of a clearly distressed soul what could have passed for a grin if it hadn't been me the grinee. Lemuel Gunn, the seeing-eye sleuth, nothing escapes his penetrating gaze. Who else, confronting a glorious barefoot contessa he'd never seen before, would notice that she didn't paint her toenails? Didn't bite them either.

"What's your line, Friday?"

"In a month of Sundays you'd never guess."

Without batting an eye she watched me inspect her chest. I wasn't looking for campaign ribbons. "You're not thin enough to be one of those high-fashion models, you're not thick enough to be a lady wrestler. I give up."

"I'm a bail bondsman. My name's Neppi. Ornella Neppi."

I flashed one of my aw-shucks smirks, which have a good track record in situations like this. "If the job description ends in 'man,' you're lying through a set of very pearly teeth."

"No. Hey. Really. Actually, I'm only a sometime bail bondsman. I'm sitting in for my uncle in Las Cruces who's convalescing from an ulcer operation. He didn't want the competition to get a foot in the courthouse door, so he got me to hold the fort."

The sun was wiltingly hot. I nodded toward the screen door of the mobile home. She looked at it, then back at me, trying to figure out if my intentions were honorable. (Didn't know how she could figure this out if I couldn't.) She must have reached a conclusion because she tossed a shoulder in one of those "What do I have to lose?" gestures that women own the patent to. I climbed the steps ahead of her and held the door open. Turning sideways, she passed so close to me going in I had to suck in my chest to avoid contact with her chest. (Maybe that's what "honorable" meant.) As the screen door flapped closed behind us, I scooped up a pair of khaki trousers and a T-shirt and several magazines and an empty container that had once played host to a six-pack and tossed them out of sight behind two potted plants, one of which was dead, one of which was dying. Friday deposited her silver astronaut-fabric knapsack on the deck and settled onto the curved yellow couch, then crossed her long shapely legs, tucking the unbitten toes of her left foot behind her right ankle, spread-eagling her arms along the back of the couch in a way that pushed her breasts into the fabric of her blouse. I turned up the air-conditioning a notch and ducked into the galley to fetch two bottles of cold Mexican Modelo. I padded back carrying a tray and set it down on the deck.

"You forgot the church key," she said.

"Don't need a church key," I said. I pried the two metal caps off with my fingertips—it was a trick I'd picked up in the badlands of Pakistan from local tribesmen who scraped their fingertips on coarse rocks until they were calloused and then opened beer bottles with their thumbs and fore-fingers to impress the NGO nurses. I filled two mugs with cracked ice, iced the inside of the glasses before spilling out the ice, then fussily filled the mugs with beer, careful to pour without forming a head. I handed one of the mugs to Ornella Neppi,

"I used to drink Guinness stout imported from Ireland," I remarked, settling onto the wooden trunk across from her, "but I can't seem to find it anymore. Can't find a lot of things anymore. Sometimes I think it's me, sometimes I think it's a national affliction. We seem to be settling for less these days—less beef in hamburgers, less service in restaurants, less plot in motion pictures, less grammar in sentences, less love in marriages." I hiked my glass. "To bail and to bonding, Friday. Cheers."

She looked away quickly and gnawed on her lower lip. Whatever ache she was repressing made her look like one of those brittle, cracked Wedgwood teacups my mother brought off the shelf for important guests. It struck me that my visitor was hanging on by her fingertips, though I couldn't figure out to what. It struck me that without the ache, she would have been too beautiful to be accessible.

"So I'll drink to bail," she finally agreed. What she said next seemed to float on a sigh. "To tell the truth, I'm less enthusiastic about the bonding part. Cheers."

Out in the park a long mobile home pulled by a truck with a throaty diesel engine chugged past in the direction of the interstate. "Okay, I'll bite—what do you do when you're not bail bonding, Friday?" I started kneading one of the metal beer caps between my fingers, turning the rim in toward the middle.

"Does Suzari Marionettes ring a bell? I can see it doesn't. No reason it should. That's me, Suzari Marionettes. That's my puppet company. I studied puppeteering in Italy and Japan when I was younger and organized this road company—we do schools, we do summer camps, we do private birthday parties, we do kids' TV when we luck in. I dress in black and work the puppets from behind with sticks. The repertoire includes *Pinocchio* and *Rumpelstilzchen*. So I don't suppose you're familiar with Rumpelstilzchen. He's the dwarf who spins flax into gold in exchange for the maiden's first-born child."

"Sounds like a depressing story."

She watched me working the beer cap between my fingers. "Unlike real life, it has a happy ending, Mr. Gunn."

"You manage to live off this puppeteering?"

"Almost but not quite. To make ends meet, I also do miming gigs at birthday parties." She kicked at the astronaut-fabric knapsack. "It's filled with wigs and funny eyeglasses and false noses for my various mime acts." She nodded toward the beer cap, which had been crushed into something resembling a ball. "Your fingers must be incredibly strong to do that."

I handed her the beer cap. "It isn't strength. It's anger."

She hefted it in the palm of her hand. "What are you angry about—something you've done?"

I shook my head once. "Something I didn't stop others from doing."

"You care to be more specific?"

"No."

"Mind if I keep this? It'll remind me of the power of anger."

"Be my guest."

She dropped the beer cap into the silver knapsack, tucked her toes back behind her ankle and, screwing up her face, chewed on the inside of her cheek, uncertain how to proceed. Meeting new people, deciding who you want to be with them, is never easy. The gentleman in me decided to help her over the stumbling block. "Knock off the Mr. Gunn. Call me Lemuel."

She tried it on for size. "Lemuel."

I reached over and offered a paw. She unhooked her ankle and leaned forward and took my hand in hers. Her palm
was cool, her grip firm. For the space of a suddenly endless
instant the thing she was hanging on to with her fingertips
was me. I can't honestly say I minded.

"You work real fast," she murmured.

"Life is short," I told her. "The challenge is to make it
sweet." I hung on to her hand long enough for the moment
to turn awkward. The depths of her seaweed green eyes
were alert, as if a warning buzzer had gone off in her head.
She slipped her hand free of mine with the casual ease of
someone who had perfected the fine art of keeping a space
between herself and the male of the species, and doing it
with minimum injury to his ego.

"Fact is, Lemuel, I'm in a jam."

In a sense, she was ahead of the game but this was neither
the time nor the place to educate her. We're all in a jam, all the
time, we're just too dumb to know it. We need to take our
cue from the drug dealers in Hoboken who, when they reach
twenty, go to the local undertaker and prepay their funeral
because they don't expect to live to thirty. "Why me?" I asked.

"So here's the deal: I can't afford the services of one of
those big-city detectives who charge by the hour and pad
their expense accounts. I went to the police but they laughed
me out of the station house. They have other things to do
besides hunt down people who jump bail for relatively
minor crimes, and the state is glad to add the bail money to
its coffers. I heard on my grapevine that you sometimes
take cases on spec . . ."

"What else did your grapevine tell you?"

"That you look young but talk old. That you'd been a brainy homicide detective in New Jersey before the CIA talked you into becoming some kind of spy. That you never run off at the mouth about it. That you were sent packing without a pension after an incident in Afghanistan that never made it into the newspapers. That you took the fall for following orders you couldn't prove had been given. That you were a troublemaker in a war that had enough trouble without you. That you came out west and went into the business of detecting in order to live in the style to which you wanted to become accustomed. That you're street-smart and tough and lucky and don't discourage easily. That what you do, you do well, what you don't do well, you don't do. Which is another way of saying you don't buy into the notion that if something is worth doing, it's worth doing badly."

"That's one hell of a list."

"I have a last but not least: that you charge satisfied customers ninety-five dollars a day and unsatisfied customers zero. That nobody can recall an unsatisfied customer."

"Can you attach a number to your problem?"

"I bet $125,000 of my uncle's nest egg this guy wouldn't jump bail. I worry that I'm losing the bet. I feel real awful about it."

"Just out of curiosity, you want to identify your grapevine?"

She flashed another one of those apologetic half-smiles. "Hey, I'd better not. If I tell you, you might send me packing. That's what my grapevine said. She said you were peeved at her for being too available. She said, psychologically speaking, you wore starched collars and liked ladies who liked men who opened doors for them. She said you'd been born into the wrong century."

Two

Friday's story, the reason she had turned up at the door of my mobile home, came out in disjointed bits, which I took to mean it hadn't been memorized. Here are the bits, jointed: Ten days before, the police in Las Cruces had apprehended a white male name of Emilio Gava on drug charges. Seems as if police undercover agents had caught him buying cocaine in a bar. After his arrest, Gava was allowed to make a phone call from the jailhouse. At the arraignment next morning, an out-of-state lawyer in a three-piece suit turned up to defend him. Friday described the lawyer, who went by the name of R. Russell Fontenrose, as unattractive a male as she'd ever set eyes on. He spurned an offer to plea bargain and pleaded his client not guilty even though he'd been caught with his hand in the cookie jar, as the saying goes. The judge, miffed to see a fancy-pants lawyer at the bar, set a high bail— $125,000. At which point a woman Friday took to be Gava's lady friend turned up with a deed to a condominium in East of Eden Gardens.

"Can you describe her?" I asked.

"I'm not good at describing people," Friday said.

"Try."

The lids closed over Friday's eyes as she rummaged through her memory. "She was roughly my height and build, with blonde hair that fell in bangs across her forehead."

"What about her eyes? Women always notice other women's eyes."

"The single time I saw her, which was in my uncle's office after the arraignment, she was wearing dark sunglasses." Friday was looking at me again. "Lemuel, what do you know about the intricacies of bail bonding?"

I had to admit what I knew could fit in a thimble.

"Okay. Here's the short course. Bail bondsmen—that includes bail bondswomen—require collateral for any bond over $5,000. If the collateral is real estate, they require double the amount of bail in equity. Equity is the difference between what the property is worth and the mortgage against it. A defendant's personal property is not eligible, but the deed was in the woman's name, which was Jennifer Leffler. She produced tax statements showing the property was valued at $375,000 and free and clear of mortgage, that the state and local property taxes had been paid up for the year. She paid the fee for the bond in advance in cash. I posted bail. Emilio Gava and Jennifer Leffler climbed into a utility vehicle and drove off."

"Sounds pretty cut-and-dried to me," I said. "Where's the problem?"

Friday rubbed the cold beer mug against her brow as if she was suppressing a migraine. "The trial is two weeks from today. Day before yesterday my uncle asked me if I'd checked out the deed with the county records office. I'm new at this—I'm embarrassed to say it hadn't crossed my mind. My uncle gave me the name of the clerk to call."

I saw where her story was going. "The deed turned out to be phony."

"I dialed the home phone number Emilio Gava left with me. I got a recorded announcement saying the line had been disconnected. I drove out U.S. 70 to East of Eden Gardens to look at the condominium listed on the deed. According to the concierge, Gava rented the condo from its owner, an Albuquerque real estate investment company. The condo itself was in one of those new communities that seem to spring up overnight—"

"Replete with minimalls and minigolf and all-weather tennis courts. Been there. Seen 'em."

"The Gava-Leffler condo was dark. They've obviously skipped out on the bail. Look, I know it's a needle-in-a-haystack situation, but I thought you might give it your best shot . . ."

She let the thought trail off. I nodded at her beer mug. She nodded no. I thought about her problem, and mine. Here's what I said: "The chances of tracking down a bail jumper in two weeks and bringing him back to court are slim." Here's what I didn't say: I was having the usual cash flow problems, bills were piling up. With summer not far away, the air-conditioning unit in the Once in a Blue Moon could use reconditioning. My vintage Studebaker needed four retreads and a new suspension. The Afghan orphan I'd adopted, Kubra, was winding up her first year at a junior college in

California that charged $5,500 a year tuition and another $2,500 for room and board. Then there was Friday herself, hunched forward on the couch, reaching down to absently massage the ankle of one naked foot. Touched by something in this cracked Wedgwood of a woman that was broken and needed mending, I heard myself say, "Why not?"

Her face brightened and I caught a glimpse of what she might look like without the weight of the world on her shoulders. "You'll try?"

"I'm not guaranteeing results."

She thrust a hand into her astronaut knapsack and came up with an item clipped from the back pages of the *Las Cruces Star* about the drug bust and the arraignment and release on bail of one Emilio Gava. In the article, he was described as a retired businessman. "Too bad they didn't publish a photo," I remarked.

"There was a *Star* photographer taking pictures on the courthouse steps," Friday remembered, "but I guess they didn't think Gava was a big enough fish to publish it."

I walked her through her involvement with Emilio Gava and Jennifer Leffler a second time, jotting down weights and heights and ages and hair colors, jotting down places and dates and the names of judges and bailiffs and officers of the court. I copied the address of the Las Cruces condo that she'd gotten off the phony deed. I marked down the various addresses and phone numbers where Friday could be reached. Her uncle ran his bond company out of an office on the second floor of a 1930s brick building around the corner from the Las Cruces courthouse. Ornella Neppi herself had a place in a fifties garden apartment community on the edge of Doña Ana north of Las Cruces. Suzari Marionettes operated out of a secondhand Ford van and a PO box in Doña Ana.

I snapped my spiral notebook closed. Friday stood up. "Can I use the facilities, Lemuel?"

For the life of me I couldn't imagine what facilities she was referring to. My confusion must have been draped across my face because she looked me in the eye and said, "So, hey, I need to pee."

"Uh-huh. Sorry. I'm a bit thick at times." I steered her to the bathroom at the back of the mobile home, then ducked into the bedroom to change into a pair of faded khaki slacks, a frayed but serviceable Fruit of the Loom and my running shoes without socks. I was collecting the empty beer mugs when Friday returned from the quote unquote facilities looking more delectable than a field of wild honeysuckle.

"This is quite a mobile home, Lemuel. You live in the lap of luxury. All the inlaid mahogany, all the Italian tiles— where'd you find it?"

"I bought it at a fire sale when one of those film studios in Hollywood went under. I suppose nobody wanted it because it was so big. They told me it was custom built in the thirties for Douglas Fairbanks Jr. when he was filming *The Prisoner of Zenda* on location. I think it was the first all-aluminum mobile home ever made, and a very fancy one at that. Which accounts, among other things, for what you call the facilities and I call the john."

"You like living in a mobile home?'

"When you move into a suburb you're surrounded by strangers. When you move into a mobile home park you're living with family."

I accompanied Friday outside and down the walkway to the road. "What is it about walking barefoot?" I asked.

"I love sand. I love earth. I love *the* earth. I'm frightened of leaving it. I'm superstitious about feeling the pull of gravity under my feet. It reminds me that I'm earthbound."

I searched her face. She wasn't making a joke. "That's an unusual superstition," I remarked.

"Oh, I have the usual ones, too. I'm superstitious about the number thirteen. I'm spooked by thirteen people eating at the same table, I won't set foot on the thirteenth floor of a building even if it's numbered fourteen, I won't walk on a Thirteenth Avenue or drive on an interstate numbered thirteen or take a plane on the thirteenth day of the month."

With the kind of suppleness one associates with cats, Friday slipped the sandals onto her feet, then angled her head and stared at me for a moment. "So I think I enjoyed meeting you, Lemuel," she said finally.

"You're not sure?"

There was a quick little shake of the head, a petulant curling of the Scott Fitzgerald underlip. "I'm not sure, no." Suddenly a cloud flitted across her features and she was swallowing emotions. She looked like one of those modern females wrestling with the eternal problem of how to give yourself generously and keep part of yourself back in case the giving doesn't work out. "So you never know who someone is the first time you meet them, do you, Lemuel? You only know who they want you to think they are."

"That already tells you something important." I cleared my throat. "I'll call you."

"Yes." She frowned. "Okay. Call me." She ducked into the beat-up Ford van parked in the shadow of a stand of Mexican pinyons and waved once through the open window as she drove off. I watched the Ford until it turned onto the interstate and was lost in the swarm of traffic. Why did I feel as if something important had happened? I retrieved the rake leaning against the tree and, turning back toward the Once in a Blue Moon, followed the prints of her naked feet down the pathway, raking the sand behind me as I went. It was a trick I'd picked up from an Israeli colleague in Peshawar—the Israelis raked the sand around their camp every night and then inspected the track for footprints first thing at first light.

Three

"Yo, Gunn? It's me, it's your daughter, it's your adopted progeny."

I kicked off my running shoes and settled my lean, mean six-foot carcass onto the yellow couch, the phone wedged between my right ear and the shrapnel scar on my right shoulder, my hands clasped behind my head, a moronic ear-to-ear grin plastered across my moronic face. "God damn, it's good to hear your voice, Kubra."

"It's good to hear yours, Gunn."

Since she'd gone off to junior college, my daughter's phone calls had become a regular Sunday morning feature, which was when the long distance rates were bargain basement. Thanks to strings I'd been able to pull with a former American ambassador to Kabul, Kubra had been one of the three hundred or so Afghan refugees allowed into the U.S. of A. She had registered at school under the name on her certificate of American citizenship, Kubra Ziayee, but she had signed up for courses, had introduced herself to classmates, using Gunn, which tickled me to tears. When she phoned me Sundays she called herself Gunn, and pronounced it with

a certain belligerent intensity, as if a lot of unspoken senti-
ments were hanging on the name. I got the message and it
warmed my heart, which was a part of the anatomy I seemed
to be losing touch with.

"How was your week, little lady?"

"I aced a bio exam and lucked into a part-time job with
a veterinarian named Cunningham. It's not much—I scrub
up after the dog and cat clients—but it's a foot in the door,
and it won't look bad on my application when I apply to vet
school. Besides which it'll sure help out in the cash-flow
department. Until further notice, I can make do without the
check you send every month. Mr. Cunningham's promised
to let me look over his shoulder when he performs operations.
What's up with you, Gunn? You haven't beat up on anyone
since that motorcycle cop in Santa Fe told you to keep your
hands where he could see them? Jesus, Gunn, what do you
have against keeping your hands where someone can see
them?"

I educated her, which is what you do with people you
love. "It wasn't what he said. It was *how* he said it."

"He said it the way a policeman says dialogue he memorized. Boy, did you have a hard time squirming out of that
one. You could have lost your detective license."

I had to smile. "To answer your question, I finally got
around to pumping out the septic—"

"You've been threatening to do it since Christmas. Has
any work come your way?"

"As a matter of fact, a lady bail bondsman came by with
a predicament. She posted bond on a guy who was caught

buying cocaine. She's pretty sure he's skipped. She stands to lose $125,000 if he doesn't show up for the trial."

"And you stand to gain some cash flow if he's brought in. What does the damsel in distress look like?"

I laughed into the phone. "Would you believe buck teeth, straw hair, cross-eyed with a lisp and a limp?"

"You're pulling my leg, Gunn. That's not the kind of moth that turns around your flame. Hey, don't do anything foolish, huh? I mean, don't run any risks, don't climb out on any limbs. You adopted me but I also adopted you. You're the only adopted father I have."

"There's no way you're going to lose me."

"Yeah. Well. Uh." I could hear her clearing a frog of anxiety from the back of her throat. "I met this dude—"

I swung my legs off the couch and sat up. "What *dude*? Are you—?"

"Am I what?"

"You know what. Ah, hell, Kubra, are you sleeping with him?"

"Oh, boy, what is it with adopted dads that they see their adopted daughters as eternal vestal virgins? The answer to your not very discreet question is, not yet. Get a life, Gunn. The dirty deed is bound to happen sooner or later—"

"I vote for later."

Her sweet tinsel laughter tickled my ear. "I'm not ruling out sooner."

If I couldn't reason with her, I figured I could scare her. "A day doesn't go by without another story on venereal disease turning up in the Albuquerque paper."

"I've read all those stories, Gunn. They even handed out a pamphlet in the home economics class. Statistically speaking, it's not the problem."

"Look, Kubra, the bottom line is, before you sleep with someone, get to know him. As long as he's not scoring for the sake of scoring, it can work out. I just think you're still kinda young."

I heard the groan work its way down the tube. "Jeeeez. I'm seventeen and a half a week from Tuesday."

"If you're still figuring in the halves, you're young."

"Don't tell me you never scored for the sake of scoring, Gunn."

"When I want to work up a sweat, I pump iron or septic tanks."

"Ninety-nine and forty-four one-hundredths percent pure! Darn it, Gunn, what are we fighting over? Ted and I haven't got past the handholding stage. We go dutch on milk shakes in the Campus Cave and talk about Elizabethan poetry and Oriental religions and NBA basketball. He walks me back to the dorm. We kiss in the shadows under the awning. Can you deal with that, Gunn, or you figuring on turning up with your shotgun?"

"I don't touch shotguns anymore. When I touch them they have a nasty habit of going off."

She laughed. "Love you."

"Me, too, little lady."

"Call you next Sunday. Bye."

"Next Sunday. Hey, if I'm not here, my accountant in Las Cruces will know where to find me."

I couldn't miss the snicker. "Your *accountant,* right. She's the one who scores"—another snicker—"I mean *keeps* score when your bank balance dips into the red. Neat legend. Bye for now."

"Bye."

Four

I put in a call to a photojournalist pal at the *Las Cruces Star*
named Lyle Leggett. Leggett was a thin man in his late forties who, without malice aforethought, managed to look
ten years older. It probably had a little to do with not shav-
ing. It probably had a lot to do with not caring. Several years
before, when we'd both been younger and fitter and less
concerned about mortality, I'd let Leggett, who was freelanc-
ing out of Islamabad, tag along when I slipped across the
Pakistani badlands into Afghanistan with a cargo of Kalashnikovs lashed to the sides of pack horses. At the time
some CIA genius had decided we ought to be arming friendly
tribesmen against the Taliban. (I use the word "friendly" in
its loosest sense.) Leggett sold the spread to the Associated
Press and eventually won a Columbia School of Journalism
photojournalist prize, which, true to form, he'd turned up
to collect with a tie hanging loose around his neck and the
top button of his wrinkled shirt unbuttoned. Last time our
paths crossed, in a bar around the corner from the *Star* a
year or so back, I'd been surprised how much hair Leggett

had lost. What little he had left seemed to have been pasted across his sun-peeling scalp one strand at a time.

"To what do I owe the pleasure?" Lyle asked when the switchboard finally figured out which extension to ring.

"I need a favor," I announced.

"I owe you, Gunn. Only ask."

"Twelve days ago a joker name of Emilio Gava was arraigned in the Las Cruces courthouse on charges of buying cocaine. He was released on bail. Someone from the *Star* was on the courthouse steps when he came out. That someone took a photo of the alleged perpetrator, but when the item materialized on an inside page, there was no photo attached. I'd appreciate it if I could get a copy of the photo from your morgue."

Leggett got back to me an hour and a quarter later. "Here's the deal, Gunn. I dug out the original rough layout for the page on which the item appeared. Funny part was they were going to publish a head shot with the article but pulled it at the last minute."

"To make room for an important article?"

"To make room for what we call a filler—something we shove in when we suddenly find ourselves with a hole in the page when we go to press. A friend in the city room seems to recall that the city editor received a phone call, after which he ordered the photo pulled."

"Any idea who might have called?" I asked.

I could hear Lyle laughing into his end of the conversation. "Maybe it was Gava's mother. Maybe her son is shy."

"At least that confirms there were photos taken," I said hopefully.

"Yeah, there were photos taken. We had a trainee named Gordon Comstock, naturally everyone took to calling him Flash Gordon, shooting outside the courthouse that day. Flash doesn't remember shooting anyone named Gava, but then he shot a half-dozen rolls of film. His personal notebook mentions six shots of a Gava, initial E. I checked the master log in the photo morgue. It lists an envelope under the name of Gava, initial E. When I looked in the *G* drawer, the envelope was missing. No photos, no negatives. Sorry I can't be of more help, Gunn."

"You may have helped me more than you know," I said. "So far you've only given me pieces, but they'll begin to fall into place. They almost always do."

"Yeah, sure. Say, if you're planning to run some Kalashnikovs across a border anytime soon, give me a heads-up."

Five

Detective Awlson sat hunched over an IBM electric type-writer, hunting and pecking away with two forefingers faster than any touch typist I'd ever seen. Every now and then he'd raise his squinty brown eyes to read what he'd written, all the while tugging at an earlobe which looked as if it'd been tugged at before. He'd frown at the mystery of the little ball stabbing typed letters onto the page, then go back to the keyboard. "What can I do you?" he asked without looking up or letting up.

I hauled one of my Santa Fe All-State Indemnity cards out of my billfold and dropped it on the desk. I was decked out in tan slacks and a tie and jacket and street shoes in order to give the Santa Fe logo credibility.

Awlson stopped typing long enough for his eyes to take in the printing on the card. He took his sweet time finishing what he was working on before slowly swiveling around to face me. I could see him giving me the kind of once-over you only get from a detective with a lot of flight time.

"Five foot eleven, one hundred sixty," he guessed.

"You're in the ballpark. You undershot by one inch and overshot by five pounds."

"I'm losin' my touch." Awlson gestured with a very pointed chin to a very narrow wooden chair. I scraped it over to the desk and lowered myself into it. "Lemuel Gunn," he announced with that New Mexican laziness which betrays a particular worldview, namely that people in a hurry die sooner. Lethargy, according to the gospel I picked up while running guns into Afghanistan for an employer who turned out to be as loyal as Iago, equals longevity. Awlson flipped my card over to see if anything was written on the back. He seemed disappointed when he found it blank. "I reckon I know what Santa Fe and All-State mean, but Indemnity has sure got me confounded."

"It's a fancy way of saying insurance."

"Hell, why don't you folks come right out with it instead of prevaricatin' the way you do?"

Awlson's cubbyhole of an office was at the bitter end of a long tunnel-like corridor in one of those precinct houses that are so old they ought to be declared historical monuments. The steel-and-glass warts we all know and loathe weren't even on the drawing boards when this particular police station was constructed. The floor was worn wide-board planking, the walls were wainscoted, the single window in Awlson's office was long and narrow and sashed with dark wood that had turned gray with age. The window was closed because the only things coming in from the street would have been noise and exhaust fumes mixed with hot

air. A slowly churning overhead propeller stirred the few
papers scattered around Detective Awlson's desk and the
wooden table near the door. There was a tall wooden filing
cabinet against one wall with a neatly folded peach-colored
sports jacket spilling out of an open drawer, and six or seven
old Remingtons piled one on top of the other in a corner.
Awlson himself was in suspenders and shirtsleeves, with the
sleeves rolled up above the elbows, a striped tie knotted
under a very conspicuous Adam's apple. A shoulder holster
with a long-barreled Colt Special nested in it hung from a
peg on the wall behind him.

He noticed me noticing the Remingtons. "We're keepin'
them 'gainst the day when these IBMs turn ornery. So who
you insurin' and what's it got to do with yours truly?"

"We're covering a bondsman named Neppi. His niece
posted bail on someone you arrested named Emilio Gava.
Miss Neppi thinks Gava may be about to jump bail, leaving
her holding the $125,000 bag. Turns out the condo deed
Gava's girlfriend put up to cover the bond was phony. My
company's in for half of Neppi's eventual loss, so they sent
me out to jump-start the eventual investigation. According
to the court records, you were the arresting officer."

"Damn right I was." Awlson moistened a thick thumb
on the tip of a pasty tongue and thumbed through a loose-
leaf desk calendar. "I'm also the chief prosecution witness.
Stanley Malone over at the prosecutor's office asked me to
show up in court at ten o'clock on—where the hell is it?—
uh-huh, the Friday after next Friday."

"I'd appreciate it if you could walk me through the arrest."

"Not much to walk. We staked out a joint called the Blue Grass, which is a seedy bar the other side of the tracks even though we do not have tracks in Las Cruces, if you see what I'm drivin' at. The county narcs been tryin' to close the place down for centuries but somebody knows somebody in the state capitol. At least that's my take on the situation. On or about eleven on the night of the second, the Blue Grass is dark but not so dark you cannot see once your eyes get accustomed. I am nursin' a drink at the bar. Officer Rodriguez is playin' pinball near the door. Officer DiPego is feedin' quarters into the juke which he claimed on his expense account and they refused to reimburse because they said he was listenin' to the music for his own personal pleasure. In breezes the perpetrator, who we later identified as one Emilio Gava, age forty-two. He is an American citizen but central castin' Italian, which is to say dark-skinned, lean and leathery, with what I would describe as a smirk but someone else'd likely call a smile pasted on his too-handsome face. Dark good looks, oily black hair swept back, good shoulders, narrow waist, head held at an angle as if he was hard of hearing in one ear, which it turns out he was—he'd been hit in the ear with a brick once when he tried to peddle protection on the wrong block. His eyes were busy flickin' here and there takin' in everythin'. I make him to be six foot even, one hundred seventy-five, and hit it on the nose. He is wearin' a white silk shirt buttoned up to the neck, no tie, a dark green double-breasted jacket unbuttoned."

"Was he carrying?"

"We see the open jacket and we think he may be, so we

all have got our handguns in our hands when we make the arrest, but he turns out to be clean as a whistle. Where was I? He slides into a booth in the back near the toilets across from a skinny kid with long sickle-shaped sideburns and a three-inch knife burn on one cheek. We later identified the second perpetrator as one Oropesa, Jesus, age twenty-seven, a Chicano with a record as long as Interstate 25 from here up to Santa Fe. I make the kid to be five foot seven and a half, a hundred thirty-three. In the mirror behind the bar I see him glance around nervous-like, then he slips a small rectangular-shaped package—now listed as prosecution exhibit A—across the table. The first perpetrator slides a long white envelope—prosecution exhibit B—back across the table to the kid. I nod to Officers Rodriguez and DiPego and we move in and collar them in the act."

"Did either of them resist arrest?"

Awlson smiled a razor-edged smile. It said, *You need to be real dumb to resist arrest if Sergeant Awlson is the arresting officer.*

"How'd he take it when you read him Miranda?"

"Perpetrators all have got poker faces these days, you never know what they're thinkin', do you?"

"Then what?"

"The rest is pure routine. We cuff them and bring them in and photograph them and ink-pad them and hold them overnight. We let them each make one phone call on the house. By noon the next mornin' they have both made bail and are out on the street."

"Detective Awlson, you described Gava's eyes flicking

here and there and taking in everything. Everything but you. I don't want you to take this the wrong way but if I spotted you sitting at the bar I wouldn't purchase cocaine no matter how dark the joint was."

His eyes, which up to then had been squinting, slowly opened and he looked at me as if he were seeing me for the first time. "You ask all-right questions, Gunn. You been in the indemnity racket long?"

"Long enough to notice things that are as plain as the nose on your face."

"My view is that I could pass for anythin' from a travelin' salesman to a travel agent. Officer DiPego chews gum and nods his head in time to the music for which he wasn't reimbursed, so he looks like somethin' that washed up on the tide. But Officer Rodriguez is fresh out of the police academy. He looks like an undercover detective tryin' not to look like an undercover detective. To answer your question, maybe Gava isn't as street-smart as you. To answer your question, maybe his eyes wasn't accustomed to the dark in the Blue Grass. To answer your question, I don't know the answer to your question."

"I have another question. What were you doing hanging out at the Blue Grass?"

"We had an anonymous tip that a buy had been set up for eleven that night."

"A letter?"

"A phone call."

"Phone calls are usually recorded."

He nodded carefully. "That's correct."

"Do you have any idea who supplied the tip?"

"It's not anybody I'd want to break bread with. Listen up, Gunn, you know and I know and the wall over there knows that the tipster wasn't a law-abidin' United States of America citizen who overheard a conversation somewhere and wanted to help keep New Mexico drug-free. It was someone with a grudge against one of the perpetrators. It was someone who had somethin' to gain by the arrest of one or both of the perpetrators. Gava and the Chicano kid were handed to us on a silver platter. Me, I am blue-collar, which is to say I never trust the contents of silver platters. If you want my opinion, the whole thing stinks."

"It'd sure be interesting to know who phoned in with the tip."

Detective Awlson's scornful smile made a curtain call. Fan lines spread out from the corners of his eyes. It was easy to see he'd give his right arm to know the identity of the tipster. I decided to push my luck and asked him if I could get to hear the original phone call. On the theory that if you go hog, you might as well go whole hog, I asked if I could have a copy of the phone call. I told him about drawing a blank at the *Las Cruces Star* and asked for a copy of Gava's mug shot.

Awlson let his glance drift over to the wall clock just as the minute hand thudded onto the hour. He pushed himself off the chair and shrugged his way into his shoulder holster and headed for the Records Department on the second floor. I fell in alongside him. "Nice digs you have here in Las Cruces," I remarked. "It's got lots of class."

"They're tearin' it down in the fall to make way for another of them shopping malls. As if we weren't drownin' in shopping malls. We're movin' into one of those air-conditioned glass-and-steel doohickeys downtown. Word is they're swappin' our electric typewriters for word processors. First I hear that words can be processed. Live, learn. What the hell, I'll add my IBM to the pile of Remingtons on the floor in case the newfangled computers crash, which is somethin' I'm told they do if you look cross-eyed at them."

"People in New Mexico kill for air-conditioning," I said.

Awlson shrugged. "I'm not lookin' forward to the move. Someone told me you can't pry open the windows if you wanted to." He snickered. "I s'pose they got our best interests at heart. I s'pose they don't want us jumpin' out in frustration."

Six

I deposited messages on Ornella Neppi's assorted phone numbers. She returned my call late afternoon. I did most of the talking but found myself leaving gaps between the sentences in the hope of hearing her voice. I suggested we meet at the new diner that recently opened halfway between Hatch and Las Cruces. "The word is out that the sirloins are thick as your thumb and charcoal broiled," I said.

She agreed on condition that we go dutch, which made me think of Kubra and that joker whose name escapes me going dutch at the Campus Cave. I proposed a more imaginative way of handling the bill. "You can pay for the solids," I said. "I'll pay for the liquids."

I was rewarded with a laugh.

"Does that mean yes?" I asked.

"Yes," she said, "it means yes."

On the way to the diner, I stopped at the hock shop on the street behind the Korean twenty-four-hour market and purchased a used Sony Walkman. Friday beat me to the restaurant—I spotted her Ford van parked around the side.

She didn't beat me by much—the hood over her motor was still warm to the touch. She was sitting in a booth at the back of the diner and waved when she saw me. I can't remember if I waved back. Then again I can't remember if I didn't. Her lips thinned into a hopeful smile as I slid onto the banquette across from her. "So you must have news to bring me all this way," she said.

The table top was transparent Plexiglas. I could see Friday had her sandals on. I could see she still didn't paint her toenails. I could see the thin fabric of a washed-out skirt hugging her thighs. I ordered two glasses of house punch and, producing the Walkman, slipped in a cassette. Reaching across the table, I fitted the earphones over her ears and hit the button marked PLAY so she could hear the anonymous phone call that sent Detective Awlson off to the Blue Grass to arrest Emilio Gava and the Chicano pusher. Here's what Friday heard.

> *[Male voice] "Awright, awright, I want to report a crime that's going to be committed."*
>
> *[Voice of female dispatcher] "Please state your name and give us a phone number where we can get back to you if we need to."*
>
> *"I don't got a name, I don't got a phone number. I don't want to get involved. I am just an ordinary citizen reporting a crime, is all. Take my woid for it, huh? I heard dese two jerks talking in a bar. A Chicano is selling five ounces of uncut cocaine to some guy at eleven tonight."*

*"Sir, we need to have your name. I can promise you
your identity will be protected—"*

*"You're chasing rainbows, angel. Nobody never found
a pot of gold chasing rainbows. You wanna know where
the sale is going to take place or you don't wanna know,
which is it?"*

"Sir—"

*"Awright, I have not got all night. What do you say we
put this show on the road, huh? The merchandise changes
hands at a joint called the Blue Grass in Las Cruces. At
eleven. The seller is a kid with sideburns, a Chicano. The
buyer is in his early forties, dark skin, dark hair, Italian."*

"Sir—"

"The Blue Grass in Las Cruces. At eleven."

At which point the phone line went dead. Friday handed
me back the earphones. I asked her if she recognized the
voice.

Friday nodded carefully. "I recognize the way he pro-
nounces the word 'awright.'" She turned away to stare out
the window for the time it took to clear cobwebs of confusion from her brain. When she finally turned back, she looked
like a deer pinned in the headlights of a car. "Shit," she said.
"Excuse my language." She shook her head in disbelief and
said "Shit" again. "When I posted bond for Emilio's bail, he
called me angel—it's him, it's Emilio Gava." She leaned toward me—I couldn't miss the groundswell of her breasts
visible over the bodice of her low-cut blouse—and lowered

her voice to a whisper. "Why would Emilio betray himself to the police?"

I said the obvious. "He wants to get himself arrested. He wants to be inside a jail."

She asked the obvious. "If he wants to be in jail, why is he jumping bail?" Then she leapt to what ordinarily would have been the obvious conclusion. "I know—he wants his fifteen minutes of fame. Getting arrested is one way of getting your picture in the newspapers."

"Except his picture wasn't in the newspapers," I reminded her, and I told Friday what my pal at the *Star* had said. "Just before the paper went to press someone phoned up the city editor, who pulled the picture. When my friend tried to find copies of Gava's photograph in the newspaper's morgue, they were missing. Ditto for the Las Cruces police station—the Gava file, which should have consisted of a mug shot and fingerprints, was empty."

Friday squinted in concentration. I was becoming familiar with her several moods. "Someone's protecting him!" she burst out.

"Bull's-eye, little lady."

The middle-aged waitress, her eyebrows tweezed down to two thin pencil lines, her hair parted in the middle and pulled back into twin ponytails, each one tied with a candy cane ribbon, brought our sirloins and a Chianti Classico with fake plastic straw covering the bottle. The sweater she was wearing—the restaurant was air-conditioned and cool— reeked of camphor, which reminded Friday of the summers she spent in Corsica, where she'd been sent when her grandfather was still alive. Like many Corsican peasants, he'd chewed on camphor for health reasons. "Hey, you don't ever want to cross me," Friday said. "I come from Corsican stock." She said it with laughter in her voice, but a dark cloud at the back of her eyes suggested she was not making small talk.

I kept the tone light. "Are you armed with more than the usual arsenal of female weapons?"

"I hope for your sake you never find out," she shot back. This time there was no hint of laughter in her voice, only the cloud at the back of her eyes.

Over dessert, Friday admitted she was curious to know my first impression of her. "Aside from the bare ankles," she added, "what did you see?"

"Aside from the bare ankles . . . hmmm." I bought time sipping my Chianti. "I saw a female of the species who rationed her smiles, as if the supply was limited. I saw a female of the species who seemed nostalgic for things she never experienced."

"Such as?"

I tried to make it seem like harmless banter. "Such as men who wear starched collars and open doors for ladies."

Suddenly she was very alert. "Are you making a pass at me?"

I grinned innocently. "Am I trying to become friends with you? Sure. Am I trying to get you into bed? If we become friends, that has to be a possibility over which you always have a veto. But for now, the answer is . . . no."

She polished off the wine in her glass and shook her head

no when I offered a refill. "So explain to me, if you can—how is it possible to be nostalgic for things you never experienced?"

I shrugged. "It's the human condition according to Gunn. In our mind's eye, we write scripts of the life we'd like to lead."

We were both finishing our coffee when I glanced at my Bulova and signaled for the bill. The waitress, wearing a name tag identifying her as Mildred, apologized for the odor of camphor coming from her sweater. "I only just landed this job," she explained. "The diner is chilly. I had to take my winter clothes out of mothballs and didn't have time to air them."

I added up the bill. "You charged us for two salads," I told Mildred. "We only had one salad."

The manager, a fat man who walked as if his trouser pockets were weighed down with loose change, waddled over. "Is something not right here?" he demanded.

I explained about the two salads. The manager checked the table slip and apologized profusely. "I hope you won't hold the mistake against us," he said.

"I won't as long as you don't hold it against Mildred here," I said. "It was an honest error. She's a good waitress."

Mildred flashed me a smile of gratitude.

As per our dutch treat agreement, I began to separate the liquids from the solids to see who owed what. Tongue in cheek, I tried to claim the salad dressing as well as the wine under liquids. Joining the game, Friday tried to claim the ice cubes in the house punch as well as the dinner under solids. "If you're going to be like that," I said, "I'm claiming the coffee." "If you're claiming the coffee," she retorted, "I'm claiming the cubes of sugar you put in yours."

We ended up laughing to beat the band. Heads turned, people began to stare at us, which only made us laugh harder.

It was our first conspiracy.

On the way out, I pointedly held the door open for Friday. In the parking lot, she very formally thanked me for the liquids. Picking up on her tone, I formally thanked her for the solids. "I'm glad you suggested a slow-food place," she said. "It gives us time to get to know each other."

"Fast food," I informed her, warming to the subject, "is the tip of the iceberg. Everything these days is fast food. You can reheat chicken in a microwave in seconds, you can get a divorce in twenty-four hours, you can keep up with the sun if you fly the Atlantic from east to west. People climb into the sack with each other without courting. There is no time to salivate over anything anymore. Salivating is an important part of enjoying the meal."

Friday fetched a key from her front pocket of the silver astronaut knapsack and unlocked the door of the van. She turned back toward me. "I did enjoy meeting you after all, Lemuel," she announced, again with great solemnity.

"The last time you raised the subject you seemed to have doubts," I noted.

"So a girl's allowed to change her mind," she said. She leaned toward me and deposited a weightless kiss in the general vicinity of my lips. Was it me engaging in wishful thinking or was this a hint of things to come?

Seven

I called Awlson the next morning to tell him the bail bonds-lady thought she recognized the voice on the phone. "You're not going to believe this," I said. "She thinks Gava fingered himself."

Awlson was unfazed. "I've been in this line of work long enough to believe anythin'," he told me. "Listen up, Gunn, all hell's broken loose since you was here. I tracked down the cop who was on the mornin' shift in Records. He says an individual flashin' a laminated FBI card turned up, pulled the mug shot and prints from the day file, signed the ledger with an unreadable scrawl, and disappeared. The captain is liftin' off like one of those souped-up rockets at Cape Ca-naveral. He phoned up the Albuquerque office of the FBI but they claim they don't know anythin' 'bout an agent comin' out here to Las Cruces and takin' records. They claim they never heard of anyone named Gava, Emilio."

I was digesting this when he said, "I seem to be addicted to dead ends these days."

"What am I missing here, Detective?"

"I ran the name Leffler past our Records people. They've

already upgraded to computers, though from the blank look on the face of the lady running that shop I'm not convinced this would come under the heading of progress. For what it's worth, the search engine—that's what they call it, I'm not making this up—drew a blank. There was no Leffler, initial J for Jennifer, listed. She doesn't have a police record. She doesn't have a bank account. She doesn't have a driver's license or a hunting license or a mortgage or a passport or a kidney transplant. She doesn't have a phone number. She hasn't paid local, state, or federal taxes. There are seventeen Lefflers, initial J for Jennifer, who carry Social Security cards. Twelve of them are drawing retirement checks, three are under seventeen, one resides in Alaska, one is recently deceased."

"Consider the possibility that she's one of those individuals with a low profile."

"Consider the possibility that she's one of those individuals with no profile."

"She exists," I insisted. "My client spoke to her the day she posted bail for Gava."

"Your client spoke to someone claiming to be Leffler, J for Jennifer. If the aforementioned Leffler posted a phony guarantee for the bail, chances are she did it under a phony identity."

"Thanks for sharing your dead ends. Made my day."

"My pleasure. What's your next move, Gunn?"

"I think I'll meander out to the Blue Grass for starters. While I'm at it I might as well take a peep at Gava's condo and see what I can see."

Eight

I lowered myself onto a bar stool at the Blue Grass that had been polished by so many rear ends you could see your reflection in it. The bartender, who wore a badge over the pocket of his short-sleeved bowling shirt identifying him as D.D., was a scrawny young man in his middle twenties with hunched shoulders and shoulder-length hair tied back to keep it out of his sunken eye sockets. He wore a small silver ring in the lobe of his left ear and had a stubble of a goatee on his chin that looked more like an oversight than something someone would cultivate intentionally. A wrinkled smile that had been worn too many times without laundering was pasted on his face. He set a chilled bottle of Dos Equis, a Mexican dark lager, on the bar in front of me. It was not yet dark outside but dark enough inside for the neon lights to be flickering on. The Blue Grass was deserted except for me and three wash-and-wear suits, traveling salesmen from the look of them, drinking Chardonnay at a corner table. D.D. wasn't against having a conversation with a customer, he just had to be egged on to hold up his half of it. A cigarette glued to his lower lip bobbed when he supplied monosyllabic answers to my run-on questions. It took me three beers to get him to loosen up.

It turned out that D.D. was not really a professional bartender. He'd taken a bartending course when he was a student at the University of Santa Cruz in California in order to pick up loose change at fraternity parties. Fact was, D.D. was a painter days and a bartender nights. If things worked out he hoped to have his first show in a Santa Fe gallery in the fall. "Painting is a lonely business," he allowed, "which is why I like bartending—I get to meet interesting folks, I get to hear interesting stories." D.D.'s hobby was inventing alcoholic drinks—mixing ingredients in a way that nobody had thought of before. His ambition in life, if ambition is the right word for it, was to give his name to a drink that swept the country. "Imagine," he said, "someone coming through them doors right here in the Blue Grass, right now, and ordering up a D.D. Dillinger on cracked ice with a twist of lime."

"What's a D.D. Dillinger?" I asked.

"Don't know," he said. "Haven't invented it yet. Working on it."

I learned, halfway through my third Dos Equis, that D.D. had been working the night the Las Cruces cops busted two clients for cocaine. "It must have been getting on near eleven," he said, leaning back with his back against one of those old crank-operated cash registers. "This Chicano-looking dude installs hisself in a booth near the lavatory. Pretty soon an Italian-looking dude with slicked-back hair ambles in. He waits by the door until his eyes get used to the dark, at which

point he spots the Chicano in the back. He asks me to
bring him a Scotch on the rocks and slides into the booth
across from the aforementioned Chicano. I bring over the
Scotch. The Chicano is already drinking tap beer. I ask him
if he wants a refill. Never lifting his eyes off the Italian he
tells me to get lost, which is easier said than done in a bar
this size." I laughed at D.D.'s little joke. He nodded happily
and laughed at my laughter. "All the while," he went on,
"there are these three dudes hanging out, one at the bar, one
at the pinball machine, one at the jukebox. The one at the bar,
the one at the pinball, are obviously cops, you have to be blind
or dumb not to make them, they came in separately but kept
checking each other out of the corner of their eye. Next thing
I know the three of them has got enormous guns in their
fists and are closing in on the booth. The Chicano starts to
jabber in high-pitched Chicano but the Italian-looking
dude doesn't look all that surprised. He angles his head off
to one side and smiles like as if he knows something nobody
else knows. The cops snap cuffs on their wrists and head for
the door. I yell after them, 'Hey, who pays for the drinks
they drank?' The Italian-looking dude seems to get a kick
out of the situation, you would never guess he is on his way
to jail. He gets the cop in the peach sports jacket to lift this
leather billfold out of the inside breast pocket of his green
jacket. Then he pulls a crisp twenty out of it and folds it like
a paper aeroplane and sails it over to me. The four road warriors and the two hookers at the long table near the door
applaud. No kidding. I remember the Italian-looking dude
saying something like 'Keep your seat belt on when you fly,

kid. Keep the change, too, awright?' I figure it takes all kinds, don't it? I mean, here is this dude being busted for possession, you have got to know they are going to go and give him serious time for that, and he doesn't forget to tip the bartender. Go figure."

Nine

If the original Garden of Eden was anything like East of Eden Gardens in Las Cruces, old Adam and his overcurious ribmate, Eve, were lucky to get evicted. Set back behind a no-nonsense chain-link fence topped with coils of army surplus concertina wire—for all I know there could have been a minefield, too—East of Eden Gardens was advertised as the promoters' vision of what paradise must be like, except when you checked the register, you noticed the promoters didn't actually live there themselves. Smart folks. Picture paper-thin semiattached white stucco condos set at weird angles to each other. Picture patches of Astroturf between the walkways, which were named after deceased movie stars. Picture a communal swimming pool inevitably shaped to look like the most fragile part of a promoter's body, the kidney. Picture two fluorescent orange all-weather Astroclay tennis courts with neon night-lights designed to attract as wide a variety of insects as possible. Throw in a Jacuzzi in every (pardon the expression) facility, a Porsche convertible or its kissing cousin in every garage, around-the-clock security with (as the signs planted like Burma-Shave ads every twenty yards promised) an ARMED RESPONSE. All this and electricity, too.

An overweight security guard wearing aviator sunglasses and a skintight blue uniform faithfully following the contours of his beer belly flagged down my Studebaker at the gatehouse to this penal colony of the spirit. I cracked the window enough to let a blast of hot air in and one of my Santa Fe All-State cards out. The guard ducked back into his air-conditioned mole hole and ran a pudgy thumb down the typed list on a clipboard hanging on the wall next to the indicators monitoring the burglar alarms in every dwelling. He leaned toward the microphone on the counter. His voice boomed at me from a speaker suspended under the roof. "Mr. Epley is expecting you," it said. "Park in the visitors lot behind the tennis courts, take Humphrey Bogart Lane on down to the first intersection, hang a right on John Wayne Way, Mr. Epley is the second garden apartment on the right. The entrance is around to the side. You can't miss it. There's a sign that says CONCIERGE on the door."

I made a mental note to ask my resident expert on the proper pronunciation of "touché" how a French Canadian would say "concierge."

Six minutes later I was rapping my knuckles on the CON-CIERGE sign. After a moment the door opened the width of a safety chain and two dark little beady eyes were giving me the once-over. "I'm looking for Alvin Epley," I announced in my Santa Fe All-State drawl.

"Who's asking for him?"

"My name's Gunn. I phoned you earlier—it's about one of your tenants, Emilio Gava."

"Yeah, I remember. You a cop or something? If so, you're wasting your time and mine. Cops already been here."

"I'm an insurance investigator, Mr. Epley. Santa Fe All-State Indemnity?" I figured if I pronounced the words with a question mark at the end, he'd assume he was the only person East of Eden who wasn't familiar with the firm. "I'd take it as a personal favor if you could help me pin down a few loose ends."

He scratched his fingernails along an unshaven cheek while he mulled it over, then shut the door enough to un-latch the safety chain and let me in. He closed the door and safety-chained it behind him. The promoters, who sold these condos starting at $99,999 for two glorious sun-drenched rooms without a view and rented out the ones they couldn't unload at $550 a month, certainly weren't pampering their concierge. Alvin Epley lived in a space large enough for four Ping-Pong tables, and it contained everything a body could ask for except space. There was a kitchenette that made my galley in the Once in a Blue Moon look like Julia Child's dream kitchen. There was a folding bridge table with four folding bridge chairs around it. There were two calendars tacked to the sooty walls, one with a photograph of the Eiffel Tower being built for the Paris Exposition near the end of the nineteenth century (which, according to Ornella Nep-pi's nameless grapevine, was the century I was meant to live in), the other with a reproduction of a painting of the Last

Supper by an Italian name of Veronese. Add two single iron beds set at right angles to each other, one made, the other stripped down to the mattress. There were two Salvation Army–modern easy chairs facing the biggest color television set I'd ever set eyes on. Also a linoleum floor with what had to be the gaudiest pattern this side of the Mississippi.

A lady newscaster with a mane of blazing orange hair and a smear of matching orange lipstick where her mouth would normally have been was describing the arrest of a father accused of administering electric shocks to his sons, aged eleven and nine, with an electric dog collar. The screen filled with a handheld shot of a stumpy man wearing baggy Bermuda shorts and a T-shirt with the words CHILDREN SHOULD BE SEEN AND NOT HEARD across it being hustled out of a police van. "They was disobedient," he shouted at the reporter thrusting a microphone in his face, "is why I did it. I sure didn't mean to hurt them none."

Alvin Epley, who looked to be fifty and then some and had the pasty complexion of someone who spent most of his waking hours sleeping indoors, waved me toward one of the two Salvation Army chairs. "Getting so you can't discipline your own children no more," he muttered. He grabbed a piece of chalk hanging from a string and made a tick next to an item on the blackboard screwed to the back of the door—I could make out *3G: feed cat twice a day* and *12B: leak under sink*. Settling into the other easy chair, Alvin zapped the TV, leaving the image on but turning off the sound. Throughout our conversation he kept his eyes glued to the screen. I wondered if he could lip-read what was being said. I noticed a plate filled with food on the bridge table.

"I apologize if I'm interrupting your meal."

"I can heat it up again, no sweat. My old lady always said things tasted better second time 'round than the first, tasted better third time 'round than the second. The meat loaf I'm eating, she cooked it up and froze it two weeks ago Wednesday, which was one day before she went into the hospital and three days before she passed on."

"Hey, I'm really sorry."

"No sweat."

"How long were you married?"

"Twenty-three years next October seven. The way I see it, we all got to go sometime. Wilhelmina was like that—she needed to be positive in her head I wouldn't go hungry before she'd let them wheel her in for the operation. She cooked up a storm for two days. I figure I still got enough to last me through the end of the month."

I couldn't resist asking him if he felt funny eating food that had been prepared by someone who was no longer among the living. With his eye still on the TV screen, Alvin hiked one bony shoulder. "We wear clothes dead people wore, we sleep in beds dead people slept in, we spend money dead people earned, why shouldn't we eat food dead people cooked?"

"You have a point."

"You know, the cops was out here asking about Emilio the day after they busted him. It came as quite a shock. Emilio was the quiet type, he kept a low profile, you know what I mean? Aside from the regular Sunday night poker game, nobody saw much of him. The cops, they had this search warrant, so I got out the passkey and neutralized the alarm and let them in his condo, which is 17C overlooking the tennis courts. Nothing much I can tell you that I didn't tell them."

"How long had Mr. Gava been living in East of Eden Gardens?"

"He turned up out of the blue eight months to the day before they incarcerated him. He was renting on a month-to-month contract because the promoters have got the apartment up for sale."

"Did you know that Mr. Gava was released on bail?"

"Little Leon, he's the guy that let you through the front gate, told me he read it in the *Star*. If Emilio was released on bail, he didn't come back here."

"How can you be sure of that, Mr. Epley?"

"The motherboard you maybe seen at the gatehouse automatically records the time a day, the day a week when the burglar alarms are set and when they are unset. A couple of days after I heard Emilio'd been released on bail, it hit me I hadn't seen him around none, so I checked out of curiosity. The alarm'd been set at twenty-two twenty—you understand military hours, Mr. Gain?—the night Emilio was busted. Except for the cops coming and going the next day, nobody else'd been in or out."

"My name's Gunn, not Gain."

"Sure. Gunn. Sorry about that."

"No harm done." I couldn't miss that Alvin kept refer-

ring to Gava by his first name, Emilio. "I take it you were kind of friendly with Mr. Gava."

"I'm Alvin to all the folks who live at East of Eden. And they're on a first-name basis with me. They all need favors— they got birds to feed or toilets that leak or doors that squeak, just this morning I had a lady who lost a pearl earring down a drain—so the first thing they do after they move in, they tip me and put the relationship onto a first-name basis to show me how equal they think I am, as if I didn't already have this information."

"Did Mr. Gava live alone, Mr. Epley?"

"He lived alone except when he didn't live alone."

"You want to spell that out?"

"Maybe two, maybe three times a week he'd turn up with a blonde, close the shutters, you'd hear funny noises coming from his place. Once the lady in 17D complained, so I phoned up and asked Emilio real polite-like to turn the music down. He said he wasn't playing music. I said maybe he ought to. Next day I found an envelope with two brand-new twenties in it stuffed through my mail slot and a note that said something about how he appreciated a concierge with a sense of humor."

"Did Mr. Gava turn up with the same woman all the time?"

"She was always blonde. Whether the same woman was under the blonde hair I can't promise. She came late and left early. She wore dark glasses even at night and a lot of lipstick."

"Does the name Leffler mean anything to you, Mr. Epley? Jennifer Leffler?"

"Nothing whatsoever."

"You said something about funny noises coming from Emilio's apartment. What kind of noises were you referring to?"

"Lookit, different folks have got different strokes. Emilio's strokes were maybe rougher than the next guy's but she was a consenting adult, so who am I to judge?"

"Are you saying he beat her up?"

Alvin zapped the TV and changed stations. He fell on a program about Hollywood sex scandals. "Maybe he beat her up, maybe she made noises like as if she was being beaten up."

"Could you give me a peek at Emilio's apartment, Mr. Epley?"

He finally turned to look at me. His eyes struck me as being very sad. Suddenly, eating food cooked by your late and obviously lamented wife struck me as a primitive but appropriate way of mourning her loss. "What exactly is it you're insuring that you need to see his apartment?" he asked.

"My company's insuring the bond that Mr. Gava appears to have run out on."

This seemed to confuse him. "The bail bondsman insures that he's going to show up for the trial. You insure the bail bondsman. Next thing, someone'll be knocking on my door and tell me he's insuring you."

"Mr. Gava was right about your having a sense of humor."

He accepted this with a nod. "I'm a laugh a minute. Look, there's no purpose me showing you 17C. Place was sold to a Jewish-type lady from Los Angeles day before yesterday, so we moved Emilio's stuff, what there was of it, into storage."

"What exactly was there?"

"A queen-size double bed, a couch, chairs, lamps, a color TV, pots and pans and kitchen glasses and dishes, a sugar jar filled with sugar swiped from restaurants, a matchbox filled with toothpicks swiped from restaurants."

"How did you know the toothpicks were swiped?"

"They was packaged two to a package and the restaurant's name was on the paper."

"Clothing? Toothbrush? Underarm deodorant? Razor?"

A photograph of a famous actress who had been caught sunbathing in her birthday suit on the Riviera came on the screen, with black rectangles blocking out her breasts and pubic hair. Alvin turned back to the TV. I watched closely but I couldn't detect a flicker of interest in his lidded eyes. "Nothing like clothes or toothbrushes," he said. "Nothing like that. Nothing personal."

"One more question and I think that'll be it." I slipped a small spiral notebook and ballpoint pen out of my pocket. "Can you tell me who Mr. Gava played poker with Sunday nights?"

"Sure I can. There was Frank Uzzel in 4B, there was Mitch Tredwell in 14B, there was Hank Kugler and his wife, Millie, in 8D. Who else was there? There was Mrs. Hillslip in 9A—her Christian name is Harriet but everyone, don't ask me why, calls her Hattie. Last but not least, not counting Emilio, was Cal Pringle in 16B and C, he bought both condos and knocked down the wall between them."

I apologized again for interrupting his meal and thanked Mr. Epley for his help. "Call me Alvin," he said. "Everyone does." He slipped the meat loaf into the microwave and turned the knob, which began to tick like a time bomb as it wound down. Then he saw me to the door. "You find Emilio, you give him regards from Alvin, huh? Tell him to keep the music turned down, he'll get a laugh outa that."

Ten

I touched base with Detective Awlson from a phone booth off Interstate 25. I had to shout into the mouthpiece to be heard over the din of the cars and trucks. I asked Awlson to pull the phone logs on Emilio Gava's home phone in 17C at East of Eden Gardens and see who Gava called. "I'm one jump ahead of you," Awlson said. "I got the phone company to send me the logs the day you told me it looked as if Gava'd skipped out on his bail."

"So who'd he call?" I asked.

"A Las Cruces pizza delivery joint, a dry-cleanin' emporium, a neighbor at East of Eden name of Frank Uzzel, another neighbor name of Harriet Hillslip, a Chicano restaurant in San Miguel, an Italian restaurant up the road in Deming."

"That doesn't give us much to go on," I remarked.

"What you need to do, Gunn, is stop by the station house. By happenstance I have someone in my office who, like the Brits like to say, may be able to help you with your inquiries."

Twenty-five minutes later I made my way down the tunnel-like corridor to Awlson's door, which was ajar. I walked in to find Awlson grilling a rail-thin Chicano with sickle-shaped sideburns and a three-inch knife burn on one cheek. "Je-sus, Jesus, you got to come up with a better story than that if you want to save yourself grief," Awlson was saying.

Awlson noticed me at the door. "Well, look what the breeze blew in—if it ain't Santa Fe All-State Indemnity in the flesh. You two know each other? Didn't think so. The jerk with the handcuffs on his wrists is Jesus Oropesa, the pusher who was arrested with that Gava fella at the Blue Grass. He was picked up this morning peddling crack outside a Las Cruces high school. Say, remember when I told you he was five foot seven and a half, a hundred thirty-three? Turns out he's three-quarters of an inch shorter but I hit his weight on the nose."

"Ever see a picture called *The Incredible Shrinking Man*?" I asked. "Maybe Jesus here *was* five foot seven and a half. Maybe he's shorter because he got zapped by nuclear fallout like that guy in the movie," I said with a straight face.

"May be," Awlson agreed.

"Which of you's the good cop?" Jesus asked with a smirk. "I been through this wringer before."

"He thinks we're gonna play good cop, bad cop." Awlson said. He seemed amused—how else would you explain the little wrinkles that fanned out from the corners of his eyes? "I ought to try it out one of these days. I know cops who swear by the good cop, bad cop routine."

"Which role you see yourself playing?" I asked.

"S'pose I'd have to cast myself as the bad cop. No two-bit pusher would fall for me being the good cop."

Jesus swallowed a yawn. "How's about you go ahead and

book me," he said. "The sooner you book me, the sooner I get to see the judge. The sooner I get to see the judge, the sooner I waltz outa here on bail. I got a mouthpiece with a big mouth, he'll plea bargain me into a two-to-five. Prisons being overcrowded like they is, I'll be walking in three, four months. The way I see it, it's a paid vacation."

Awlson shook his head in disgust. "The syndicate that employs these jerks pays them monthly salaries while they're doin' time as long as they don't name names."

"Mind if I ask him a few questions?"

"Why would I mind?" Awlson said. "I need to relieve myself." I grinned. He grinned back and left the room, closing the door behind him.

I settled onto the edge of Awlson's desk. "I need to clear up some details about the arrest at the Blue Grass."

"I do not know nothing 'bout nothing," Jesus said.

"Did you ever do business with Emilio Gava before the Blue Grass?"

Jesus only smirked.

"Who set up the buy that night? Emilio Gava himself?"

The smirk was pasted on his face. I could feel the anger that resided permanently in my fingertips rising through my arm and on up to my throat.

"Was there a go-between? A woman maybe?"

"You know what you can do with your fucking questions," Jesus said with a smirk. "You can shove them up your fucking ass."

I lost it. *It* being my cool. *It* being my dignity. I ducked behind him and jerked the handcuffs and his wrists upward.

Jesus shrieked "Police brutality" but I only laughed under my breath and pulled his wrists higher. "I'm not a cop," I told him, "so this can't be construed as police brutality." I experienced a surge of pure pleasure as I elevated the cuffs another increment. I could feel the arm sockets in his shoulder reaching their limit before I reached my limit. Tears were streaming from Jesus's eyes as he gasped, "Go ahead, break my arms, even if I knew who set up the sale, which I don't, I wouldn't tell you because they'd break my balls."

I released my grip on the cuffs and took several deep gulps of air to calm myself. I had come off adrenaline highs before, namely in Afghanistan, so I was not surprised by the free fall. When I could talk again, I said, "Let's say for argument's sake you're telling the truth for the first time in your life. How could a guy like Gava, who is not local, score cocaine in this town?"

Jesus was breathing hard. "He must have called the right number and named the right names."

"Was he a junkie?"

"Christ no. The minute I seen him coming through the door, I could see he was not a user of the cocaine he was buying. You can spot users a mile off—they got this gleam in their eyes, they got dilated pupils, they can't wait to pay you off and get their hot hands on the shit. When you finally pass it over they're like kiddies in a candy store. Gava was laid-back like an undertaker at a funeral. I figured right off he was buying for a friend."

"Or buying in order to get caught in the act."

"You are one crazy hombre, you know it? Why would

somebody in his right mind set up a buy to get caught in the act?"

"What if I told you the police were tipped off about the sale in the Blue Grass? What if I told you that a third party has identified the voice tipping off the police as Gava's?"

"You got a wild imagination," Jesus said. "You ought to go and write movie pictures."

Later, with Jesus safely back in the holding pen, I took Awlson to a local bar for a beer. "What did you find out?" he asked.

"I found out his arms bend back more than most people's. I found out I'm not in the right line of work—I ought to be writing scripts for films."

Awlson was one of those old-fashioned cops who learned the trade before electric typewriters existed. He flipped open a small notebook and set it down on the table. He uncapped a thick fountain pen, the kind that sucks up ink from an inkwell, the kind that he might have gotten for a birthday present when he graduated from high school. "Let us summarize the situation," he suggested.

"We are dealing with a joker who moved into the East of Eden Gardens eight months ago and kept a low profile," I said.

Awlson moistened the ball of a thumb and flicked through the notebook to another page. "He ordered in from a pizza joint, he ate out once in a while, he played poker with neighbors Sunday nights, he shacked up two, maybe three times a week with a blonde who made funny noises during sexual intercourse."

"Now I know who interviewed Alvin Epley before me,"
I said. I picked up the thread of the summary. "Then, seem-
ingly out of the blue, Emilio Gava sets up a purchase of cocaine, after which he puts in an anonymous call to the
police to make sure he would be nabbed in the act."

"After his arrest," Awlson went on, "he makes a single
phone call from the police station. The next morning a big-
city lawyer turns up to plead him not guilty. At which point
Gava is released on bail and disappears into the woodwork."
Awlson raised his eyes, his mouth scrunched up in thought.
"If he wanted to disappear, why didn't he just up and disappear? Why did he have to go to all the trouble of getting
himself arrested for buying cocaine?"

We both nursed our beers thinking about this. Finally I
said, "Gava needed to disappear in a way that made it look
as if he had a good reason to disappear. He wanted someone
or some organization to think he was running away from a
drug conviction and jail sentence. Which must mean he had
another reason to disappear but wanted to mask it."

"Maybe Jesus was right after all," Awlson said. "Maybe
you ought to write for the movies."

"If we can figure out *why* Gava wanted to disappear," I
said, "maybe we can figure out where he disappeared to."

Out on the sidewalk, Awlson offered a hand. He hadn't
done this before with me. I shook it. "I didn't fall for your
Santa Fe All-State Indemnity crap," he remarked.

"Didn't think you would," I said. "At least not for long.
But we're on the same page when it comes to bail jumpers."

He thought about that. "Yes and no. You're a private eye.

You've got a client who needs to find this Gava clown before I do."

I shrugged. "Sorry I didn't come clean."

He shrugged back. "What's next on your Santa Fe All-State Indemnity agenda?" he asked.

"I probably ought to have a heart-to-heart talk with the out-of-state lawyer who turned up to spring Emilio Gava."

Eleven

On a porcelain-brittle morning I wedged myself into a seat between a pasty-faced anesthetist returning from a tax-deductible medical convention and a waif-woman who could have passed for female from the neck up but looked like a twelve-year-old boy from the neck down. Coming into Chicago, with the wheels about to graze the tarmac, the three of us were scared out of our skins when the plane was clobbered by a sudden rainsquall and wind shear. Gunning both engines so hard the wings seemed to flap like a bird's, the pilot circled around for a second go. I mention this because the fright I experienced was nothing compared to the mortal terror I felt when, an hour and a quarter later, an aluminum space capsule moonlighting as an elevator whisked me up eighteen—count them, eighteen—floors without my realizing it had even moved. The thing that gave it away was the decor. On the ground floor I'd been gazing dumbly out at another bank of elevators and a fancy sign that said CRESS-WELL BUILDING. When the doors slipped soundlessly open a few moments later, I assumed I'd see the same bank of elevators and reached over to punch eighteen again. Instead I found myself staring at a silver wall with giant silver letters on it that read FONTENROSE & FONTENROSE. A wispy brunette with streaks of silver in her teased hair ("Receptionist wanted, experience helpful, silver streaks in hair a must") and enough mascara to ballast a pocket battleship was holding fort behind an aluminum table in front of the wall. Coming at her from the side, I could make out a very short and very tight skirt and a pair of very knobby knees. The receptionist tore her eyes away from her fashion magazine with an obvious effort.

"Talk about coincidences," I said. "That girl in that picture"—I twisted my head so I could make out the page she was reading right side up—"I was sitting next to her in the plane this morning."

"You have got to be kidding! I'd give up not smoking to meet Julia Crab. What was she like?"

"Don't know. She put a mask over her eyes and slept the whole way. The only time she said anything was when we almost crashed. What she said was not something I can repeat to a lady." I leaned over the desk and lowered my voice as if I were sharing a state secret. "I'm here to see Mr. Fontenrose."

"I could have guessed that," she purred, eyeing me with interest. "We're the only ones on the floor. Which Mr. Fontenrose?"

"How many are there?"

"Seven, not including the two sons-in-law with different last names."

"R. Russell is my man."

"Whom shall I announce?" she asked with a slightly breathless Marilyn Monroe lisp.

"DSC Lemuel Gunn."

She screwed up her mouth in disbelief. "And what, pardon the prying, does the DSC stand for?"

"Deputy station chief, darling, which happens to have been the last rank I held before the Central Intelligence Agency fired me for conduct unbecoming."

As her pointed bosom thrashed around inside a blouse that had been bought one size too small or had shrunk in the wash, she directed me to an enormous leather couch and then stabbed at numbers on her house phone. There was a shoelace-high aluminum-and-glass table in front of the couch with copies of an economic review set out on it like cards in a game of solitaire. I flipped through one to pass the time. It was filled with pages of graphs showing that if the money supply got tighter, interest rates would get looser. Or was it the other way around? Either or, I didn't understand a word. France-Marie, my lady accountant in Las Cruces, would have felt right at home.

After what seemed like an eternity, a well-groomed older woman with white hair tied up in a bun and one ankle bound in an ACE bandage limped through a door I hadn't noticed the existence of. She lowered her head, a gesture that suddenly added a second chin to the one she already had, and sized me up over the silver rims of large oval eyeglasses. I was wearing faded khakis, loafers without socks, and a threadbare sports jacket over a particularly shabby sports shirt that I was very attached to because the collar didn't chafe my neck.

Apparently my attire brought out the latent arrogance in her. "Naughty, naughty," she purred, wagging an accusing finger. "You haven't phoned ahead to make an appointment, Mr. Gunn."

"Who are you, dear lady?"

"My name is Miss Godshall. I am the secretary to Miss Wyman, who is the principal secretary to R. Russell Fontenrose. If you care to state your business, perhaps I can put you out of your misery."

"Are you a trained attorney?"

"I am a trained secretary. I am trained to spot people who are unable to afford three hundred dollars an hour to talk with the gentleman who employs me."

"Look, Miss Godshall, why don't you duck back through your secret door and tell Miss Wyman to tell R. Russell that Lemuel Gunn has come all the way up from Las Cruces, New Mexico, to talk to him about a bail jumper name of Emilio Gava. I lay you odds he'll squeeze me in."

Pouting in disapproval, Miss Godshall raised her head in a huff, reducing her chins to the number God had distributed at birth, pivoted on the heel of a sensible flat-soled lace-up shoe and limped back through the secret door. Five minutes later I was ushered into the presence of Miss Wyman, a tall, elegant, flat-chested woman who looked like the dowager madam of a high-class brothel. Her hair was dyed red but I suspected it was already rusty underneath. Miss

Wyman, in turn, ushered me into the presence of the man himself, R. Russell Fontenrose.

His corner office came with wraparound windows double glazed to keep out everything except the sob of sirens, and even those sounded as if they came from another planet. The room was so vast I thought I'd need a motorized golf cart to get across it before he went out for his two-martini expense account lunch. Picture ankle-thick wall-to-wall carpet. Picture a king-sized mahogany desk. Work in the usual family photographs in the usual mother-of-pearl frames, a small Chinese bowl filled with monogrammed matchbooks, the usual law books in the usual leather bindings, a collection of antique globes on a long low glass shelf. Don't forget to include the smell of saddle soap and furniture polish and money. Especially money. Through a partly open door, I caught a glimpse of a minigym—a rowing contraption, a pile of towels, a set of golf clubs. On one side of his desk was an electronic monitor listing the waiting phone calls, which were stacked up like jetliners in a holding pattern. R. Russell was perched against the edge of his desk, his back toward me, murmuring into a telephone. "I've laid the options out for him, Kenneth. He can snipe at them from the safety of the trees with writs of this and that, which will slow them down but won't stop them. Or he can grab the bull by the horns and sue the trousers off them for breach of contract and watch them squirm." He noticed my reflection in the window behind his desk. "I have someone with me. Let me get back to you." He hung up and dog-paddled around to the front of the desk to get a better look at me, during which time I got a better look at him. R. Russell was an ungainly man—wide waist, broad chest, broad in the beam—in his late thirties or early forties. Neither his seventy-five-dollar haircut nor his nine-hundred-dollar suit could disguise the fact that he was seriously ugly, which is how Ornella Neppi, who'd seen him that one time in court, had described him. He had fat jowls and beetle brows and tiny eyes and a gnarled nose, all of which gave him the allure of a hagfish, which is one of those eel-like creatures you come across now and then in the Bermuda Triangle. If you're lucky, you come across it when it's dead. Its most distinctive feature is a mouth filled with horn-shaped teeth for boring through the flesh of fishes in order to feed off their innards. For some reason I couldn't put my finger on, this accumulation of ugliness only seemed to make R. Russell very, very sure of himself. I'd run into people like him before—they think, for their ship to come in, they only have to put to sea. He didn't offer to shake hands. Neither did I. He glanced at a wafer-thin wristwatch that he wore on the inside of a fleshy wrist. I supposed he was checking the time so he could bill me later.

"Your secretary's secretary told me you get three hundred bucks an hour."

"That's correct." He gave me the once-over, guessing the size of my bank balance from the cut of my trousers. I was very fit and reasonably tan, both attributes that come in two basic models—playboy prosperous or down-on-his-luck indigent. It was easy to see which he had me pegged for.

"The three hundred an hour put me off," I admitted. "I was worried you couldn't be much good at what you do if that's all you charged."

He didn't crack a smile. He didn't even look as if he had one in his inventory of expressions. "Perhaps you ought to get to the point. I'm a busy man. What's this about Emilio Gava jumping bail? And what does it have to do with you?"

"I represent the Neppi bail bond company, which stands to lose $125,000 if Emilio Gava doesn't turn up for his trial. We have reason to believe he skipped out on his bond. He never returned to his condo in Las Cruces after you pleaded him not guilty. Nobody seems to have any idea where he is or how to get in touch with him. Being his lawyer, I thought you might have an address or a phone number."

"Are you familiar with the legal concept of attorney-client privilege, Mr.—what did you say your name was?"

"Gunn. Lemuel Gunn. I've heard of attorney-client privilege but I thought, all things considered, you might waive it in Mr. Gava's case and give me a helping hand. As his attorney, you are also an officer of the court. You asked the judge to release Gava on bail. As I understand it, it's not in your interests to have him jump bail."

R. Russell stabbed at the sleeve of his jacket and took another look at his watch. "Thank you for stopping by, Mr. Gunn. I'm sorry I can't be of assistance to you. Now, if you don't mind, I'll have my secretary show you to the elevator."

"I do mind." The horns of our stares locked. "In fact, I mind a great deal. I came a long way to see you. It would be a blow to my ego to have to go home empty-handed." I drifted over to the glass shelf running along one wall and absently plucked one of the antique globes off of its cradle.

"Be careful with that—it's a three-hundred-year-old Lorenzo da Silva. It's worth more than you earn in ten years. There are only three da Silvas in the world in anything like this condition—the second is in the Louvre, the third is in the Metropolitan. I'll sue the trousers off you if you so much as scratch it."

"I don't know much about law but I know enough to know the difference between actionable and collectable. If I were to drop this—always assuming the judge doesn't buy my story that you tried to physically throw me out of your office and the globe got busted in the altercation—you could sue the trousers off me, as you put it. But as I own nothing in the way of equity, and as my bank balance, last time I looked, was in the neighborhood of minus seven hundred and fifty dollars, the only thing you'd collect would be my trousers. I'm not sure they'd go with your haircut, Mr. Fontenrose."

"I could attach your income for the rest of your life."

I tossed the globe from my right hand to my left and then back again. I could hear him suck in his breath. "I don't have an income," I explained. "I don't go to an office, I don't draw a salary. How about it, Russell? All I want are simple answers to simple questions."

I gave the globe a spin and tried balancing it on the tip of my middle finger. "For Christ's sake put it down," he whispered hoarsely. "I'll tell you what I can."

I kept the globe in the palm of my hand just in case. "Who hired you to represent Emilio Gava?"

He made his way around his desk and collapsed into a leather chair that appeared to fold itself around him. "Our firm has an ongoing relationship with—" He sucked air in through his nostrils and started over again. "Over the years Fontenrose & Fontenrose has taken on some special clients— we deal with their legal problems, we manage their financial portfolios." His hagfish mouth clamped shut. He was clearly having a hard time spitting it out. I played catch, left hand to right hand and back again, with his three-hundred-year-old Lorenzo da Silva. He groaned. "This is the first time one of our special clients has been arrested after going into the program. Certainly no one in the program has ever jumped bail—"

"What program are we talking about?"

"The Federal Bureau of Investigation's witness protection program. That's as much as you're going to get out of me, Mr. Gunn. If you require more information, I suggest you go to the horse's mouth."

"Would you care to identify the horse's mouth?"

"Talk to Charles Coffin. He runs the witness protection program for the western states out of the FBI's Albuquerque office."

I could actually hear his sigh of relief when I deposited his precious globe back in its cradle.

"Please leave now, Mr. Gunn."

I looked at my watch. "Twelve minutes. Which means I owe you one-sixth of three hundred dollars, which is fifty bucks." I pulled two twenties and an Alexander Hamilton from my billfold and dropped them onto his king-sized desk. "That makes us even-steven, pal."

I plowed through the carpet to the door. Miss Wyman led me down the corridor to Miss Godshall, who led me back through the secret door to the elevators. Heading back toward earth in one of the Cresswell Building's silver time capsules, I felt like a sap for having paid for Fontenrose's twelve minutes. As gestures go, it'd been pretty dumb—I was out of pocket fifty bucks, all to feel superior to an eel.

In the words of D.D. back at the Blue Grass, go figure.

Twelve

Ever since the honcho himself, J. Edgar Hoover, fired an agent he spotted in the hallway for wearing tight trousers, every FBI field office that I've been to has been an island of haberdashery conformity. The New Mexico field office, on Luecking Park Avenue in downtown Albuquerque, was certainly no exception. The men circulating in the corridor sported dark two-piece suits with button-down shirts and conservative ties. The two female secretaries at the main desk wore jackets that flared at the hips over sober dresses that plunged to midcalf. Maybe it was my imagination working overtime, but even the men on the Ten Most Wanted list posted on the wall next to the elevator seemed comparatively well decked out, which made me wonder if casual apparel like mine could keep you off the Most Wanted list. The way the secretaries sized me up, I wondered if casual apparel could keep you out of the New Mexico field office.

"There's no agent here by the name of Coffin," the older of the two secretaries informed me with nasal finality.

"I have it on good authority that the agent in question,

one Charles Coffin, runs the FBI's western witness protection program out of this field office," I persisted.

"Everything all right here, Miss Pershing?" a two-piece suit passing the reception desk asked.

"Gentleman here seems to think we have a Mr. Coffee working out of this office," the second secretary said.

"Mr. Coffin," I corrected her. "Charles Coffin."

"Sir, who are you?" the two-piece suit demanded.

I reached into my hip pocket for my wallet to come up with some ID.

"Sir, I need you to keep your hands where I can see them," the two-piece suit said. The pleasant smile never quit his lips.

"Last time someone told me that, we wound up having an altercation," I said.

"Sir, is an altercation anything like a fight?"

"It starts off with insults. It moves on to pushing and shoving. Where it ends depends on the parties involved."

A second two-piece suit materialized in a nearby doorway. I wondered if the secretaries had little buttons under the rim of the reception desk that they could push if someone with casual apparel turned up on the premises.

"What's going on here?" the second agent demanded.

"This . . . *gentleman* . . . wants to see an Agent Coffee," the second secretary said.

"Coffin," I corrected her, "as in casket. Coffin as in sarcophagus. He's supposed to be the agent in charge of the FBI's witness protection program in this neck of the American woods."

The second agent circled around me. "Are you a police officer?" he asked.

"I'm a private investigator—"

"You possess identification?" the second agent asked.

I pulled back the flap of my threadbare sports jacket and,
moving in slow motion, extracted the wallet from my hip
pocket. I produced my laminated New Mexico detective license from the wallet and waved it in the air. The first agent
snatched it from my fingers. "Goes by the name of Lemuel
Gunn," he told his colleague. "State-certified private investigator working out of Hatch."

"A real private investigator, in the flesh," said the second
agent. "We haven't seen one of those fellers around here in a
coon's age."

"Listen," I said, "if you don't have a Charles Coffin working out of this field office, you must have a witness protection program."

"I've read about witness protection programs in detective
novels," the second agent allowed, "but I've never actually
seen one on FBI premises."

"Sir, you fixing on joining the witness protection program?" the first agent asked.

"I'm trying to track down someone who I have reason to
believe was in your witness protection program. His name
is Emilio Gava. He was released on bail after being charged
with buying cocaine. I have reason to believe he has no intention of turning up for the trial."

"Which would make him a bail jumper," the first agent
said.

"Bail jumpers are a police matter, aren't they?" the second agent asked the first agent. He eyed me. "Have you tried the local police in the jurisdiction where you expect him to jump bail?"

I wedged my wallet back into my hip pocket. "I don't have much experience with the FBI, but if all their agents are like you jokers, the country is in deep shit," I said.

"Sir, I need you to watch your language," the first agent said. "There are ladies present."

"Language isn't something you can watch," I shot back. "To get the full impact, you need to hear it."

For some reason the second agent repeated my name. "Lemuel Gunn, with two *n*'s."

"Sir, is there anything else we can do for you?" the first agent inquired.

"As a matter of fact there is. Can one of you Bobbsey Twins direct me to a good tailor in Albuquerque? I'd kill for a two-piece outfit like the ones you're sporting."

I got to say this for me, I live and learn. At least this time it didn't cost me fifty bucks to feel superior.

Thirteen

Lady Godiva riding bareback couldn't have lured me back to that promoter's idea of kingdom come, East of Eden Gardens, but Ornella Neppi's predicament could and did. It wasn't my style to leave a body unburied or a stone unturned. I decided to chat up Emilio Gava's poker partners in the hope of eliciting a heretofore overlooked detail, a snatch of conversation, who knows, maybe even a lead to the occasional blonde bombshell who turned up at Gava's condo, obliging him to turn up the radio. In short, I was scrounging for anything that might help me pick up the cold trail of the presumptive bail jumper.

Frank Uzzel in 4B was the first name on the list I'd gotten from the concierge, Alvin Epley. I pushed the doorbell expecting a buzzer, what I heard were chimes playing the first notes of "The Stars and Stripes Forever." A thin, very young Chicano maid wearing a starched white apron and suffering from terminal acne cracked the door. "You the man what called?"

"I am the man," I said, flashing the grin I used to disarm civilians.

"If it's that Allstate fellow, Consuelo, show him in," a voice called from another room. "I'm expecting him."

Uzzel turned out to be a square-jawed, crew-cut, gray-haired retiree with ramrod posture, standing or sitting. He wore a short-sleeved polo shirt and had a dog tag tattooed across the biceps of his left arm. (I recognized it because I used to wear two of them around my neck.) He looked to be one of those veterans who had married into the army the way priests marry into the church, he looked like he intended to remain faithful to his dying breath. He received me in a den one wall of which was covered with photographs of him in combat fatigues, another with a gun rack filled with as lethal an arsenal as I'd come across outside of a forward base armory. "I made top sergeant," he allowed, following my gaze, looking at his photographs as if he were seeing them for the first time. "Thirty-three God-wonderful years in the finest military on Mother Earth. Four of them in Nam." He motioned me to a chair next to a glassed-in case filled with medals, each one set on a small purple pincushion. "You serve your country, Mr. Gunn?"

"I think I did, yes," I said.

"Where'bouts?"

"Afghanistan."

He pursed his lips respectfully, one soldier acknowledging another. "I hear tell Ghanistan wasn't a picnic."

"No one who was there would describe it as a picnic," I agreed.

"Did I hear you right? You *thought* you'd served your country? Jeez, how can you not be sure?"

I hiked one shoulder. "Military service is complicated," I said. I glanced at the photos on the wall. "I'm sure you can relate to that. You do what you're told to do. You do it as well as you can. Sometimes it works out, other times it doesn't."

"Nam was sure as heck complicated," Uzzel said. "I was never sure which of the turkeys in black pajamas was the enemy and which was on our side, so I treated any turkey in pajamas as a potential hostile. Hostiles sometimes wound up dead before they could convince us they weren't hostile. Heck, in Nam I was never sure what a victory would look like, though I got to admit I sure recognized defeat when I looked it in the eye."

I nodded. "Afghanistan's not all that different," I said. I waved away his offer of a Scotch neat, then accepted when he insisted. He poured one for himself and settled onto an ottoman covered in camouflage tent cloth.

"This is about Emilio, huh? That's what you said on the phone."

It turned out that Gava's arrest had been a hot item of scuttlebutt in the East of Eden rumor mill. I explained about the suspicion that he intended to jump bail. "I heard he sat in on your regular Sunday night poker game, so you must have known him. I thought you might remember something he said—a comment, a quip, anything at all—that could help me find him so that my company doesn't have to reimburse the bail bondsman who'll have to fork over $125,000 to the state."

"Jeez, I don't know as how I can add much to what you already know. Our poker game'd been running for years when Emilio moved into Eden. Hattie Hillslip over in 9A, she's the one who went and invited him to join our Sunday night shootout. That's what we call it. A shootout, though needless to say no guns are allowed at the table." Uzzel chortled (Kubra's pet word these days; she claims I don't laugh, I chortle) at a private joke.

"What?"

"Emilio knew I was a gun collector from when he played here at my place," Uzzel said. "He knew we had this little no-guns-at-the-table rule. It was one of those little rules you joke about but everyone figures is sensible. So one night, we were playing at Hank and Millie Kugler's over in 8D, Emilio all of a sudden produced the neatest little two-shot derringer I ever set eyes on, and I've set eyes on my share. It was so small you could conceal it in the palm of your hand and nobody would be the wiser."

"How did your Sunday night regulars react to this breach of etiquette?"

"Heck, we all laughed. What else was there to do?"

"I see what you're saying," I said.

"What am I saying?"

"You're saying you don't confront a man with a weapon in the palm of his hand."

"Jeez, you're putting words I never spoke in my mouth. You're putting thoughts I never thought in my head."

I tried to change the subject. "How do you decide who gets to host the game any given week?"

Uzzel let go of the previous subject reluctantly. "We take turns. One dollar is set aside from every pot to pay for the whisky and beer and cold cuts and potato chips and salted peanuts. I got to say, Emilio enjoyed the poker. He was in his element. The way he shuffled cards, the way he dealt them, he could have been a professional dealer in a previous incarnation."

"What was he in this incarnation?"

"Don't know as anybody ever asked him. He was Italian, you know, not that there's anything wrong with being Italian. But those heavy lids that closed over his eyes didn't encourage personal questions."

"Generally speaking, did he win or lose?"

"Off the top of my head, I'd say he won more than he lost."

"Especially when he was dealing," I ventured.

Uzzel angled his head to squint at me. "What makes you say that, Mr. Gunn?"

"Your description of the way he handled cards. I've seen dealers who can shuffle till you say stop and then make four aces come off the top every eighth card."

"Yeah, well, don't think the thought didn't occur to us—"

"But the heavy lids closing over his eye didn't invite accusations of cheating."

"If he'd been caught at it, I wouldn't have backed off, I would have challenged him, derringer or not."

"I believe you would have, Mr. Uzzel. Did Gava ever host your shootout?"

"He took his turn in the lineup like everyone. Three, maybe four times, sure."

"Did anything out of the ordinary happen when he was the host?"

Uzzel gave this some thought. "I remember the phone ringing one night when we were playing at Emilio's condo. He let it ring for so long it interrupted the game. Everyone stared at Emilio. Emilio stared at the phone, which was ringing off its hook. 'Jeez, answer it,' I said. Emilio scraped back his chair and got up and plucked the phone off the hook. He listened for a few seconds, then he turned his back on us and spat out in an angry whisper"—here Uzzel actually lowered his voice to an angry whisper and did his best to imitate Gava—" 'This is not a good time to call me, awright? I got company.' "

"He said 'Awright'?"

"That's the way he pronounced 'all right.' Awright. We laughed about it when we were playing tennis next day."

"We?"

"Hattie Hillslip over in 9A. Her Christian name is Harriet but everyone, don't ask me why, calls her Hattie."

"How did the phone conversation end?"

"Emilio has sure got hisself a temper—it ended with him hanging up so hard I was sure he must have busted the phone."

The Chicano maid appeared at the door, which was ajar. "I'm off marketing, Mr. Uzzel."

"Don't forget the cranberry juice, Consuelo. Lots of it." He turned back to me. "You like cranberry juice, Mr. Gunn?"

"I don't think I ever tasted it."

"You ought to. Filled with vitamin A. Calcium. Ascorbic acid. 'Course, there's more vitamin A in raw cherries but not as much ascorbic." He laughed in embarrassment. "I'm a fitness nut. Jog eight, ten miles every morning even in the rain."

I pushed myself to my feet. "You've been generous with your time, Mr. Uzzel. Can I hit you with one last question?"

He stood, too. "Why not?"

"Ever catch a glimpse of Gava's lady friend?"

A queer smile spread across Uzzel's square jaw. "Matter of fact, spotted her a few times when I was jogging on John Wayne Way before breakfast. Coming out of Emilio's street. Blonde like one of them blonde movie stars. Enormous sunglasses which covered half her face. I reckoned she was wearing them because she wanted to be incognito. She wore one of those long raincoats even though it wasn't raining so I didn't get a good look at her body. But I'll bet she came equipped with a good figure—heck, you can pretty much tell if a lady has got a good figure from the way she moves. She got into a panel truck parked in the visitors lot behind the tennis courts and drove off."

"Did you notice what kind of panel truck? The make? The color?"

Uzzel scratched his head. " 'Fraid not. 'Fraid I was more interested in the lady than the vehicle."

After Uzzel, I tried the Kuglers. I was curious to hear their version of the derringer story. I pushed the bell on 8D expecting music. Instead I heard a human voice yell, "Who the hell is it?" Go figure. I was wondering whether the pro-

moters had thrown in Uzzel's John Philip Sousa with the
condo when Millie Kugler answered the door. "I'm the All-
state guy who called from the gatehouse," I said. I grinned
and held out my hand knowing she'd have a hard time refus-
ing it. Get someone to shake hands with you, you have one
foot in the door. Kugler was out playing golf and Millie
seemed only too pleased to have a visitor elbow into the mo-
notony of her day. Her condo was crammed with *stuff*—
cushions with the names of cities embroidered on them,
statuettes of naked ladies and the Eiffel Tower, antique irons,
antique candlesticks that had been electrified, antique hulls
of model antique ships with dust collecting on their antique
sails. Looking around, it struck me that she had enough pos-
sessions to furnish a second condominium. Millie herself was
a seriously overweight, big-breasted woman in her middle
sixties who had had, to my eye, one face-lift too many, which
accounted for the tautness of the skin around her eyes and
mouth, which explained why the only smile she could mus-
ter appeared pained. Her dyed hair was set in permanent
waves on her scalp and looked something like frozen groundswells on a great lake. I could see right off she'd once turned
heads when she walked into a room. She could see that I
could see, which is probably why she shrugged before I could
ask my first question. I suspected all of her conversations
began with a shrug. It was her way of leaving unsayable things
unsaid.

It turned out that she, too, had heard about Gava's arrest,
but on her rumor mill he'd been selling cocaine, not buying.
Yes indeed, she recalled the night when he'd produced the

derringer. "One instant those long beautiful fingers of his were empty, the next, hocus-pocus, he was holding this tiny handgun in the palm of his hand. It was so small I thought it had to be a toy. He was laughing to beat the band. I think he'd put more than his share of bourbon under his belt because once he started laughing he seemed to have trouble stopping."

"Knew a woman once who said she couldn't cry—said she was afraid once she started she'd never be able to stop."

"What's that got to do with me?"

She was defending a border that hadn't been attacked. "Just trying to make small talk," I said lamely.

"Cut to the chase, Mr. Gunn."

I cut to the chase.

Yes, she recalled the night he'd gotten a phone call when he was playing host to the shootout crowd. In her memory, Gava referred to the caller by name. "It was either Annette or Annabel," Millie Kugler said. "I have difficulty placing faces when they're out of context but I never forget a name. The phone call impressed everyone because it revealed a side of Emilio we'd never seen. Normally, he was a pussycat, the flirtatious neighbor eager as the next man to casually brush the back of his wrist against your bosom. I lost count of the times he went out of his way to carry my shopping bags from the trunk of my car into my kitchen. The one or two times I saw him angry, his eyes seemed to go dead. Oh, I heard from Alvin—you ought to talk to him, he's the concierge here at East of Eden—about Emilio's blonde bimbo. Alvin is always passing on the latest rumor. We joke that he's the host of a morning gossip program called *Radio Eden*. Alvin let everyone know that Emilio had to turn up the volume of the radio to drown out the racket of their hanky-panky. Shoot, when we were younger, Hank and I used to turn up the radio, too. Twice a day on a good day."

"Did you ever set eyes on Gava's blonde visitor?"

Millie shook her head. "The way Alvin tells it, she turned up after my bedtime and departed at the crack of."

"Emilio ever give you cause to think he wasn't happy here?"

Millie turned to stare out the window. Several people in tennis shorts were cutting across her lawn heading for the courts. "I need Alvin to put up a DON'T WALK ON THE ASTROTURF sign." She turned back to me. "What were you saying?"

"Did Gava seem to you to be happy here?"

"What are you suggesting, Mr. Gunn? That he's not a bail jumper after all but a fugitive from a retirement Gulag?" She guffawed at her own little joke. "To answer your question, nobody's *happy* here. This is a gated senior community. This is a pearly-gated predeath community. The reason no one is happy here is that no one here is young anymore. Shoot, you need to be young to be happy anywhere."

"Gava was only forty-two."

She favored me with one of her pained smiles. "Maybe he felt uncomfortable around fogies. I know I do, even if I'm one of the fogies. Truth is, I wasn't surprised to hear Emilio had upped and disappeared."

"What makes you say that?"

"Emilio looked and acted like someone who'd been sentenced to East of Eden."

"You want to go and spell that out?"

"When my Hank was in the navy—oh my, *tempus* certainly does *fugit,* that was forty-two, forty-three years ago—he was forever counting how many days he had left before his discharge. It used to drive me up the wall. He was a short-timer who counted time. He'd cross off the days on a calendar. I had the eerie feeling Emilio was counting days like my Hank. If he didn't cross off days on an actual calendar, he was sure as shoot crossing them off in his head. He was forever asking what date it was. I'd say, to give you a for instance, that it was the twenty-fifth and he'd say something about March being almost over and summer being just around the corner. If Emilio winds up jumping bail like you think, trust me, trust a woman's intuition, it's because his time here was up."

I was running out of poker players to interview. According to Alvin Epley, Mitch Tredwell in 14B was off on a Mediterranean cruise, Cal Pringle in 16B and C had gone to the Mayo Clinic in Baltimore for his annual medical checkup. Which left Harriet Hillslip, the woman who brought Gava into the Sunday night shootout. I called her from the gatehouse to introduce myself. "Don't need more insurance," she said when she caught my Allstate spiel. "Canceled my life insurance after my third divorce, didn't want to give the son of a bitch of an ex a motive to kill me."

"I'm not selling insurance," I assured her. "I was hoping to ask you some questions about Emilio Gava."

"Hello? Emilio the bail jumper?"

"Word spreads fast in East of Eden."

Mrs. Hillslip in the flesh was a handsome woman in her early fifties who shared a condo with her old mother. You couldn't help but notice that Mrs. Hillslip had a shapely figure—she was wearing a ribbed chest-clinging sweater and jeans so tight it made a feller wonder how she got into them in the morning, how she got out of them at night, always assuming she got out of them at night. She perused my business card. "Knew a Lemuel once. Must have been when I worked in South Carolina in real estate. Lemuel Gulliver I think his name was. Or was that a character in something I read?" She shook her head to clear out the cobwebs. "You-all call me Hattie, Lemuel," she simpered as she let me in. "Everyone around Eden does. *Mother!*" she hollered at the old woman rocking in a wooden rocking chair watching a television quiz show with the sound turned off, *"we have got a visitor."* The old woman never turned her head. "She's hard of hearing," Hattie explained as she led the way into a small kitchenette, "which is why we never bother turning up the sound on the TV. Deafness can be a blessing, Lemuel. Mother watches television most of her waking hours. Before she became deaf she used to watch it with the sound turned way up. Drove me half crazy."

"Does she read lips?" I asked.

"She reads minds," Hattie said matter-of-factly. "It's downright disconcerting. She always seems to know what I'm going to say before I write it down on her pad." She settled onto one of the designer metal stools set around the egg-shaped table. I sat on another stool across from her. "Coffee, tea or me," she said, her fingers on my wrist. She laughed when she saw my expression change to confused. "Shoot, only kidding." She sat back and eyed me. "You look too savvy to be an insurance salesman, Lemuel. What is it you really sell?"

"Services," I said.

"I'll take a wild guess. You-all exterminate rodents."

I had to smile grimly at how close she'd come. "I hunted down rodents in my day. I let the people I worked for do the exterminating."

"You're not joking, are you?" The tip of her tongue flicked at her upper lip. "So that's what brings you to East of Eden," she said. "Is Emilio Gava the rodent you're after?"

I smiled away her question. Prodded by my occasional interjections, Hattie warmed to the subject of Emilio Gava. "Fact is, our paths crossed more often than the other players in our poker shootout."

"How's that?"

"First time he sat in on the weekly shootout in my condo, he noticed that my phone had one of those unit counters attached to it—it's right there on the counter behind you. I'd more or less inherited it from the previous owners, along with everything electric, since they were moving to the south of France where none of this stuff would work. Anyhow, Emilio took me aside one night and asked if he could come by now and then to use my phone."

"Did he give a reason?"

"He said something about being harassed by the IRS for

something a business partner of his did. He thought the government might be tapping his phone line."

"How often did he use your phone?"

"Oh, he didn't take advantage. Maybe once or twice a week. He'd come by when I was off shopping and bring Mother a strawberry tart he'd picked up at that French bakery in Las Cruces, along with a pile of movie magazines—Mother can spend endless hours reading movie magazines when she's not watching TV. When I came back from my shopping, I'd find a scrap of paper on the kitchen table marked with how many units he'd used, along with the money to pay for it. He always left more than enough and never let me make change. If he was still here when I got back, I'd invite him to stay for dinner. Sometimes he accepted."

"Do you remember how many telephone units he used?" I asked.

"Dear me, it was usually somewhere between twenty and thirty, though once he must have had a long-winded conversation because he left enough money to pay for a hundred and seventeen units."

I steered the conversation off on a tangent. "Did you ever hear strange sounds coming from Emilio's apartment?"

Hattie retreated behind a sly smile. "Don't think I don't know why you're asking that. Alvin's been telling everyone who'd listen he'd had complaints from Emilio's immediate neighbors. Live and let live is my adage. Did you know that in certain states anything but the missionary position is against the law? Shoot, what consenting adults do in the privacy of a boudoir is their business.

Besides which, nobody forced her to come back to the
condo with him."

When I got up to leave, Hattie's old mother was still glued
to the TV set. She'd removed her dentures and put them in
a glass of water next to her chair. When she laughed, she was
all gums.

Hattie's hand was on my upper arm when I turned back
to her at the door to thank her for her time. "You're welcome
to stay for dinner," she said. Once again her face was draped
with that sly smile. "You're welcome to stay for dessert," she
added. "I'm the dessert, Lemuel darlin'. I don't hold with
the state law about missionaries dictating what's legal and
what's not. Since mother is stone deaf, we won't have to
turn up the radio."

Don't ask me why but one-night stands have always turned
me off. My immediate problem was to sidestep the invitation
without hurting her pride. "Listen, Hattie, I find you awfully
attractive—what man wouldn't? Normally I'd jump at your
invitation but the fact is, I have a medical problem."

"It's not some dreadful venereal disease?" she said breath-
lessly.

I averted my eyes.

"Oh, my poor dear Lemuel. Well, you did the honorable
thing telling me. I know a lot of men who would have climbed
into the rack anyhow."

I muttered something about taking a rain check. She nodded. I asked her for her phone number so that I could cash in
the rain check. She jotted it on a blank page of my little note-

book, then stood on her toes and kissed me on the cheek. When I looked at my face in my Studebaker's rearview mirror, I could see traces of her lipstick on my face. I wet a corner of my handkerchief with saliva and wiped them off.

Driving back to Hatch, I pulled up at the first phone booth I spotted. It reeked of urine. I took a deep breath and held it and reached in to dial Detective Awlson's private number, then stepped outside to talk. Awlson sounded cantankerous when he came on the line. "Hope you've got some good news for me," he said.

"I've got a good lead," I told him. "Gava used one of his neighbor's phones a lot—he told her he thought his phone line was being tapped by the IRS." I held my notebook up to the light and gave Awlson Hattie Hillslip's number.

"I'll pull the log from the phone company," he said.

"By the by, when you searched Gava's condo after his arrest, did you come across one of Mr. Derringer's short-barreled two-shot pistols?"

"Something told me you'd have bad news. What makes you ask?"

"Seems as if he owned one. Seems as if he showed it off to his poker-playing pals."

"To answer your question, there was no two-shot derringer in his condo."

"Which means he must've stashed it somewhere when he was choreographing his arrest. Which means he was very attached to his little cannon and planned to recuperate it when he got out of jail."

"What you're saying is he's probably armed, right? Shit, piss and corruption! If he's armed, he's dangerous."

"All rodents are dangerous," I said.

"You're going to explain that, I suppose."

"Running out of quarters," I said, and I hung up.

Fourteen

I was stretched out on my yellow couch, shoes off, feet crossed at the ankles, head on the armrest, eyes tight shut, relishing a delectably cold Carta Blanca straight from the bottle. France-Marie, my French Canadian lady accountant, was working on the Formica table in the galley—I could hear the rustle of paper as she went through my checkbook, balancing the latest monthly statement from the savings and loan folks. A Nat King Cole 33 was on the stereo. Only two of the four speakers still worked but the song—"It's Almost like Being in Love"—was making me nostalgic for things I still hoped to experience. In my nostalgia, I suppressed the image of Gava's sweet little double-barreled derringer and replaced it with Ornella Neppi's delicate footprints on my sand pathway, toes turned outward. I fantasized about the barefoot contessa who had made them.

The sound of my phone ringing startled me out of this sumptuous reverie. I reached lazily behind my head for the receiver and brought it to my ear.

"Gunn, it's me, your adopted offspring."

"I recognize your voice, little lady. What are you doing

calling Friday? I thought we were locked into Sunday phone rates."

"Calling Friday because I won't be near a phone on Sunday."

"Why's that, little lady?"

"Ted's invited me to go with him to his parents' place in the country—it's on an island on a lake, you need to have someone with a boat come pick you up from the landing."

I sat up on the couch. "Are you asking permission to go or informing me you're going?"

"Don't climb on your high horse, Gunn. Hear me out, huh?"

"I'm listening."

"You're listening but you're not *hearing*. Ted's parents and his two sisters will be there. I'm sharing a room with the sisters."

"What do his parents do?"

"They parent, for Pete's sake."

"For work, I mean."

"I think his father is a lawyer. The reason I think that is he seems to want Ted to go to law school."

"Lawyers are not my favorite people."

"Private investigators aren't all that popular with the general public either, Gunn."

"You still haven't addressed the question. You *are* asking permission to go, aren't you? I've got it right, right? That's why you called?"

A sigh from the bottom of Kubra's war-torn soul—her childhood in Afghanistan had been strewn with agonies—

reached my inner ear and I melted. "Okay, little lady, you have my permission to go even if you're not asking for it. But I have conditions. When you bunk in with the sisters, you are physically present in their room the entire night."

"I love you to death, Gunn, but I think you're a prig."

"I'm not sure what 'prig' means."

"It's a guardian of morality who thinks Mary was a virgin when she gave birth to Jesus. It's someone who thinks sexual intercourse contaminates the female of the species."

I laughed uncomfortably into the phone. There was a grain of truth to what she was saying.

"There you go, chortling again," she said.

"I'm not sure what 'chortling' means."

"Lewis Carroll invented the word—we're reading *Through the Looking-Glass* in my lit class. *O frabjous day! He chortled in his joy.* 'Chortle' is a cross between 'chuckle' and 'snort,' which is a perfect description of what you do when you laugh."

France-Marie appeared from the galley. "I've finished the savings and loan statement, Lemuel. Also the quarterly self-employed estimated tax form— all you need to do is lick a stamp and mail it in. You *can* lick your own stamps? Mind if I use the loo?"

I nodded yes. Kubra said, "Somebody there with you, Gunn?"

"My accountant's come by to do my paperwork."

"You mean your *lady* accountant. At this ungodly hour?"

"She has three clients in Hatch. The manager of the roller-skating rink. The guy who runs this mobile park. And me.

I was the last but not least on her appointed rounds, which is why she stopped by a bit late."

I could hear Kubra—how can I describe this?—chortling. "Maybe you're less of a prig than I thought," she said.

I suddenly needed to get something off my chest. "Pay attention, Kubra. Hang on my every word. Wherever you're at, however old you are, your best years are ahead of you. And don't you ever forget it."

I heard her awkward silence. Then, "You're talking to yourself, aren't you, Gunn?"

She was a smart cookie. "I'm talking to the both of us, little lady." I changed the phone to the other ear. "Bye," I said. "Have a good weekend on your island."

"Bye-bye, Gunn of my heart," she said. "Have a good night."

Smiling to myself, I put on another Nat King Cole 33 and moseyed into the galley alcove to deposit the empty beer bottle into the garbage pail. There was a half-empty wine-glass on the Formica table, along with a battery-powered adding machine. But no France-Marie.

"France-Marie?" I called.

When she didn't reply, I made my way aft, past the head, to the bedroom. The door was ajar. France-Marie was stretched out naked on my bed, her red hair enticingly splayed across one of my pillows. She watched me watching her. "Don't just stand there, honey," she said. She had left her accountant's voice in the kitchen alcove. "Come to beddy-bye."

I'm old school when it comes to intercourse, sexual and

otherwise. France-Marie and I had made love maybe a dozen times; she'd slept over twice before. She obviously expected to spend the night tonight. What could I say to let her down easily? Nothing occurred to me and I didn't want to bruise her ego, so I stripped to the skin and climbed in alongside her. She rolled onto me, pressing the length of her generously endowed body against mine, kissing me on the lips and the side of my neck, nibbling on an earlobe, sucking on one of my nipples, all the while caressing my genitalia, which couldn't have cared less about bruising the ego of an occasional lover.

France-Marie stopped abruptly. "What's wrong?"

"Nothing's wrong. I've had a hard day is all."

She went back to caressing my organ, feather-light strokes with the tips of the fingers of her left hand. I tried to summon an erection. I even resorted to subterfuge—I ordered up an image of the butter-colored sleeveless blouse plastered against several of Ornella Neppi's very spare ribs. Turned out I had as much control over my erections as I did over Kubra when she had her heart set on a weekend with her boyfriend.

France-Marie weighed my wilted weed in her hand. "There's someone else, isn't there?"

I took a deep breath. "I met a girl," I admitted.

"Have you slept with her?"

I shook my head. "We had dinner. She kissed me on the lips in the parking lot."

France-Marie rolled off me to her side of the bed and

pulled the sheet and light blanket over both of us. "Men,"
she said. "Who understands their music? Certainly not me.
At least you're honest, unlike my ex."

I slipped my arm under her and pulled her closer so that
her head was nestling into my shoulder. "Me neither, I don't
understand me," I said. "You're a fine woman, France-Marie."

After a while she whispered, "I'm not going to play second fiddle."

"I'd never ask you to."

France-Marie listened to me breathing. I listened to her
listening. I heard the bedside clock ticking away the minutes for the first time since I'd bought it, years before. I heard
an owl in the branches of a tree hooting for its mate. I heard
the occasional eighteen-wheeler on the interstate that skirted
the mobile park, which meant the prevailing wind was
coming in from the Painted Desert. In the absolute silence
between the owl and the eighteen-wheelers, I caught the faint
scruff of footfalls on my sand walkway. I'm not an Apache
but I'd swear the footfalls were made by shoes, not bare
feet.

A man's shoes.

"Where you going?" France-Marie whispered.

"To the john."

Feeling my way in the dark, I retrieved the Colt .38 Com-
mando revolver—a favorite weapon of CIA field agents—
from its hidey-hole in an old lace-up boot, pulled on a pair
of jeans and a T-shirt and padded barefoot past the head to
the small escape hatch across from the main door of the
mobile home. Easing open the two dead bolts, which I made

a point of keeping well oiled, I slipped outside and hunkered down into what my hand-to-hand instructors called a combat crouch. Tufts of cumulus clouds were defacing a sliver of a moon not bright enough to cast shadows. Moving stealthily, I made my way around the side of the Blue Moon and came up behind the figure of a man trying to peer into my mobile home through one of its windows. I jammed the business end of my Colt into his ear as if it were a Q-tip.

The Peeping Tom turned out to be a balding Caucasian male in his fifties. He was wearing a varsity jacket with the number 23 on the back, khaki trousers with pouch pockets on the sides of the legs, sturdy shoes. He froze the way children do when they're playing Red Light, Green Light. "I figured it was time for Muhammad to come to the mountain," my nocturnal visitor said lazily. He laughed under his breath. "Name's Coffin. Charlie Coffin. A little bird told me you'd been nosing around the FBI regional office looking for me."

Charlie Coffin had the street smarts of someone who had spent most of his working hours outside of an office. The business end of a Colt in his ear didn't faze him—all in a day's work, his body language seemed to say. Moving with the world-weariness of a snail crossing a leaf, he produced a laminated identity card with the letters FBI across the top and a mug shot of an agent on it. "That's me eight, maybe ten years ago," he said, gingerly easing the barrel of my Colt to one side with two fingers. "Had more hair on my head back then. You're damn good, sneaking up on me like that," Coffin said with grudging admiration. "I heard as how you'd picked up some field savvy in Afghanistan."

"Field savvy didn't keep me from getting kicked out of the Company," I said.

Coffin grunted. "Lose some, lose some others."

I took a closer look at the mug shot, then studied the face of the intruder as he slowly turned toward me. The two matched up. "You armed?" I asked.

He held up his palms. "Only with my hands," he said. "I'm a black belt karate. Could have taken you down when you went and stuck the gun in my ear. You won't take it amiss if I give you a friendly suggestion? When you get the drop on somebody, you need to keep back out of arm's reach."

"Trying to take me down could be dangerous for someone's health," I said. "Hey, you didn't come skulking around a mobile home park at night to test out my moves."

"Didn't," he agreed. "I heard tell you'd been asking 'bout Emilio Gava's connection to the witness protection program. I thought as how we needed to have a conversation."

I thumbed the safety on the Colt forward and stuck the handgun in my waistband as I led my visitor around back and into the Once in a Blue Moon through the escape hatch. The front door was bolted closed on the inside and I didn't want to rouse France-Marie from her beauty sleep. I turned up the air-conditioning and brought in two cold beers from the galley.

"Okay, Gunn. I'll begin at the beginning," Coffin said. He unzipped his varsity jacket, revealing a T-shirt with FBI in bold black letters across the chest. "To understand who Emilio Gava is you need to understand where he comes from. Just inside the Nevada state line, a few miles from Nipton,

California, which is a fleabag of a town at the edge of the Mojave Desert, there's an old stagecoach station called Clinch Corners. About eight years ago, two minor Mafia families that couldn't get a foot in the door in Vegas or Atlantic City decided to set up shop there. The result was and is two small casino operations, one on each side of what passes for a main drag, in the middle of nowhere—but only seventy-five minutes out of Los Angeles by automobile, twenty minutes by helicopter. The two families that run the two casinos, the Baldinis and the Ruggeris, avoided stepping on each other's toes until eighteen months ago when Guido Baldini, the youngest son of Giancarlo Baldini, the godfather of the Baldini family, was arrested and sent to prison for income tax evasion. The Baldinis naturally suspected that the paperwork that turned up in the FBI's hands was supplied by a member of the Ruggeri family, which happened to be not true—we got the ledgers from a disgruntled bookkeeper who thought he'd been cheated out of a year-end bonus. To get even, the Baldinis had Guido Baldini's brother Salvatore turn state's evidence, implicating the youngest son of the head of the Ruggeri clan, Fabio Ruggeri, on racketeering charges. You with me so far, Gunn?"

"A tooth-for-a-tooth situation."

"Exactly. The scheme worked. Fabio Ruggeri was sentenced to twenty-five years in a federal penitentiary, which is where he is today. Salvatore Baldini, who turned state's evidence, went into the FBI's witness protection program. We gave him a new identity and a nest egg and resettled him in Arizona, which is where I come into the picture. I run the

witness protection program for the western states. Things
back in Clinch Corners quieted down for several months and
we assumed the two families had worked out a modus vi-
vendi. Then, one day 'long about ten months ago, someone
named Silvio Restivo, a.k.a. the Wrestler, waltzed into our
Flagstaff office and offered to turn state's evidence against
Salvatore Baldini who, by this time, was safely tucked away
in our witness protection program. Silvio—he was nicknamed
'the Wrestler' because nobody could whip him at arm
wrestling—turned out to be a dealer at the Ruggeris' casino, and a cousin of the jailed Fabio Ruggeri. The Wrestler
swore on a stack of Bibles that he was the driver of the car
from which Salvatore Baldini gunned down two Italians
who had cheated the casino two years before. By law we were
required to submit the Wrestler's deposition to the grand
jury, which indicted Salvatore for murder and then demanded we bring him back from witness protection purdah
to face trial."

Coffin was one of those rare characters who could drink
and talk at the same time, as if the beer irrigated the vocal
cords. He turned his bottle upside down to show me that it
was empty. I padded into the galley and fetched him another.

"Where was I?" he demanded.

"You were being obliged to bring Salvatore back to stand
trial for murder."

"You're a good listener, Gunn. The FBI was of two minds.
The majority opinion believed the Wrestler's testimony and
felt that Salvatore was guilty and ought to be sent to prison

for life. The minority view, represented by yours truly and a handful of my associates in the Albuquerque office, thought the Wrestler's testimony stank. To us it was part of a Ruggeri plot to get even with the Baldinis for sending the youngest son up the river. For Marco Ruggeri, the godfather of the Ruggeri clan, it was a matter of family honor. If someone can betray one of theirs and get away with it, others might be tempted to do the same. Still, the law was the law, so we gift-wrapped Salvatore and delivered him to the courthouse in Flagstaff for arraignment. When Salvatore Baldini emerged from the courthouse an hour later, a sniper shooting from a roof a good half mile away put a 175-grain hollow-point boat-tail through the cornea of his right eye."

"Blinded him," I guessed.

Coffin appreciated my sense of humor. "Blinded him dead," he said.

"I vaguely remember reading about that in the paper," I said. "Which left you with Silvio 'the Wrestler' Restivo on your hands."

"Which left us with the Wrestler. Our people grilled him for weeks but if his testimony was part of a plot to lure Salvatore out of the woodwork for a rendezvous with a sniper's bullet, he never admitted it. His hotshot attorney insisted we stick to the terms of our signed agreement. We had no choice but to take him into the witness protection program."

"I'm taking a stab in the dark—that was eight months ago."

Coffin nodded. "Eight months ago we gave him a new moniker, Emilio Gava, and set him up in a condominium in East of Eden Gardens, Las Cruces. We kept close tabs on him—we tapped his phone, we tapped the public phones in and around this East of Eden that he might use—but we never discovered anything that would lead us to believe he was part of a plot to lure the late lamentable Salvatore out of hiding."

"Were you able to identify Gava's blonde girlfriend?" I asked.

He shook his head no. "He picked her up at an Italian block party off old Route 66. To the naked eye, she looked like a garden variety hooker."

By now my beer bottle was empty, too, but I wasn't in the mood for a refill. "Then you found out the Wrestler had been arrested for buying cocaine at the Blue Grass," I said.

"Gava phoned me from the police station. We're the ones who brought in R. Russell Fontenrose, from Fontenrose & Fontenrose, which is a firm we have worked with in the past—R. Russell takes care of the financial and legal affairs of people in our witness program. I reckon you know the rest of the story. The Wrestler had been caught in the act. R. Russell pleaded him not guilty and got the man you know as Emilio Gava released on bail. When I went around to East of Eden Gardens the afternoon of the arraignment, Gava had already skipped."

"Why did you yank his photos from the *Las Cruces Star* morgue, and his fingerprints and photos from the Las Cruces police station?"

"That was done by FBI agents who came down from Washington. They confiscated all files and photos of Emilio

Gava and made sure the *Star* didn't publish his picture. I don't even have one. The next-to-last thing the boys from Washington wanted was for the newspapers to splash a photo of a cocaine buyer over its front pages and have the caption identify him as someone in an FBI witness protection program. The last thing they wanted was a rehashing of the whole Clinch Corners affair. It would have led to a lot of embarrassing revelations about the FBI being manipulated by Mafia clans, so the Washington office reasoned."

I took another stab in the dark. "To avoid embarrassment and unwanted publicity, you guys were going to offer the Wrestler another new identity so he'd never stand trial. You were going to see to it that Emilio Gava disappeared from the face of the earth."

Coffin offered up a mocking grin. "Wrong by a country mile. I was going to lock him in a room and tickle the bejesus out of him until he admitted he had set up Salvatore for the sniper. I knew the cocaine thing was a phony from the word go. The Wrestler didn't use cocaine. I'll lay odds he set up the buy and then tipped off the Las Cruces cops to get himself arrested. He wanted out of the FBI witness protection program, but he needed to exit in a way that made it look as if he was running from a cocaine rap. If he'd just upped and run, those of us who thought he'd set up Salvatore for the sniper would have put him on our Ten Most Wanted list. Sooner or later we would have found him. But running out on a cocaine bust—shit, our people couldn't have cared less."

There was a long silence as I let Coffin's tale sink in. I looked up. "When Silvio 'the Wrestler' Restivo, a.k.a. Emilio

Gava, turned up in Flagstaff offering to turn state's evidence against Salvatore, what reason did he give for doing it?"

"He said he was tired of running errands for the mob, tired of dealing five-card stud five nights a week. He said he'd met a woman and wanted out. The local FBI agents verified his story—there was a woman in his life by the name of Annabel. The problem was, with the mob you have a lifetime membership. You never retire. So the Wrestler said he was taking the only way out he knew. It sounded plausible. He was offering us a killer in exchange for a one-way ticket into our witness protection program and a new life."

"Did this Annabel exist?"

Coffin nodded.

"What happened to her?"

"She disappeared from the radar screen when the born-again Emilio Gava disappeared into our program. When we asked him about it, the Wrestler intimated they had split up."

I thought some more. "Why are you laying all this out for me?"

"Good question, Gunn. The Emilio Gava file has been officially taken out of my hands. The powers that be will be happy if they never hear of him again. But not me. I am a fossilized cop—I have a silent-screen mindset. I've been in the FBI twenty-seven years. My father was FBI before me. I was brought up to believe in an abstract principle called justice. Cops bring criminals to justice. That's what we're paid for. That's how we get to kid ourselves we're doing something useful for the planet. Chances are the Wrestler did lure Salvatore into the sniper's sights. Chances are he's gone to ground in a Mafia-run witness protection program. I want you to find him. I want you to bring him back for trial. I want twenty-four hours alone with him. When I'm finished with him, the cocaine bust will be the least of his worries. I want to charge him with being an accessory to the murder of Salvatore Baldini. I want to blow the Ruggeri-Baldini feud wide open."

Coffin polished off his second beer and set the bottle down on the floor between his feet. "The place to start," he said, "is Clinch Corners."

Fifteen

Not counting the Hindu Kush, it was one of the longest nights of my life. We'd been pretending to be asleep for hours but the silence between us kept us both up—funny how you can lie next to someone not sleeping and know she's not sleeping from her breathing. When all's said, enchanting a woman is more satisfying than disenchanting her. When you disenchant her you wind up seeing yourself through her eyes. The image, to say the least, isn't agreeably familiar.

It was still dark outside when the phone ringing in the living room roused me from my awful wakefulness. "I'd better get that," I said, only too eager for an excuse to leave the bedroom. "It could be important."

France-Marie sat up on her side of the bed. "I should be going," she said. She snapped on the bed lamp and started collecting her clothing. I've noticed women have a lot of dressing to do before they can be described as dressed.

"Stay for breakfast," I said so unconvincingly the words left a bad taste in my mouth. I caught a glimpse of France-Marie's vertebrae as she reached behind to fasten her brassiere. "I'm sorry about how things turned out," I mumbled, pulling on sweatpants and a thick Afghan jersey I'd bought for a song in one of those tribal souks where they sell clothing and guns in the same stall.

"You're not sorry," she said. "You're relieved."

I didn't contradict her. Padding past what I now thought of as the facilities, I plunked myself down on the yellow couch and lifted the receiver to my ear.

"Who's this?" I demanded.

I must have come across as grumpy. "Who the hell is *this*?" the caller shot back. I recognized the gravel in Detective Awlson's growl. "It's me, Awlson," he said. "You don't sound none like that Allstate fellow I know," he added. "What'd I do, interrupt a wet dream?"

"I don't do dreams, wet or otherwise," I said. "Don't regret not. Dreams would probably put a damper on an otherwise all-right day."

"You dream dreams, pal—everyone does. You only don't remember them." I could hear Awlson's impatient snort on the line. "I got my hands on the phone company logs," he said. "You curious to hear what I found?"

"For Pete's sake," I said.

"They were sure interesting," Awlson said. "Someone made nine phone calls from Harriet Hillslip's number to Nevada, to a bar in the town of Searchlight name of the Original Searchlight Speakeasy Saloon. That mean anything to you, Gunn?"

"It will," I said. I settled back into the couch and told Awlson what I'd learned from Charlie Coffin the night before. "Your Emilio Gava is really Silvio 'the Wrestler' Restivo, a

Ruggeri family member who turned state's evidence to lure Salvatore Baldini out of the FBI's witness protection program, at which point Salvatore was knocked off by a sniper."

"I remember the hit," he said. "I remember thinking the shooter was one hell of a good shot. The whole business didn't strike me as kosher at the time, but local cops don't score career points second-guessing the FBI."

Inside the Once in a Blue Moon, a toilet flushed. A moment later the front door opened. I called out, "Let's keep in touch." France-Marie must have heard me because she called back, "Let's" just before the front door slammed shut hard enough to stress-test the hinges.

"You talking to me?" Awlson said on the phone.

"I was talking to a passing fancy," I said. "About the Wrestler," I went on, "turns out he had a girlfriend name of Annabel. Could be that she was working at the Searchlight Speakeasy Saloon. Could be that Gava was keeping in touch with her from Harriet Hillslip's kitchen phone."

"Could be," Awlson agreed. "What you figuring on doing next, Gunn?"

"I'm going to shower and shave and percolate up a pot of Maxwell House. Then I'm going to find Friday—"

"Come again?"

"Friday's my nickname for Ornella Neppi, the lady bail bondsman who put up the $125K so Gava could get out of your jail. Stay tuned."

"Tuned is my permanent state. Listen, next time I get you out of bed with important information try to sound halfway human when you come on the horn."

I had to laugh. "I'll keep that in mind," I said.

I dialed Ornella's number in Doña Ana and let the phone ring a dozen, fifteen times but there was no answer. I put in a call to Ornella Neppi's uncle, the Neppi in Las Cruces who was recovering from an ulcer operation. "I know who you are," he said when I spelled my name—I get hot under the collar when people spell it with one *n* as in "weapon." "Ornella told me all about you, including your trying to sweet-talk her into bed."

"She said that!"

"Didn't need to. Wasn't born yesterday, Gunn with two *n*'s. I can spot your type a mile off." He put a hand over the mouthpiece and said something to somebody about appreciating bacon with his French toast. He came back on the line. "Make no mistake, Ornella's a fine girl. She's had her ups and downs when it comes to men. Treat her nice-like or you'll have me breathing down your neck."

"I'll treat her real nice," I promised. "Now tell me where I can find her? She's not answering her home phone."

Turned out Suzari Marionettes was performing in a Pueblo youth club up north in Taos. I headed for my Studebaker parked in a stand of shady trees behind the Once in a Blue Moon, checked the oil and tire pressure. I threw my small canvas overnight bag into the backseat, fitted the key into the ignition, pulled out the choke and pushed the starter button. Remember cars when they had chokes and starter buttons? The car backfired only once before the motor coughed into life. I eased her down the dirt path and turned into the road—only to find myself sandwiched between a hulking black SUV and a sleek off-white vintage Cadillac. Car doors opened. Three goons appeared from the SUV and closed in on my Studebaker, walking with the lazy body language of professional bouncers. The fourth man, short, thickset, impeccably dressed in a double-breasted three-piece suit the same color as the Cadillac, approached from the other direction. He wore a fedora and thick, perfectly round glasses that magnified his eyes for anyone on the outside looking in. He gestured for me to roll down my window. I rolled it down partway. He leaned closer. "We hear you are looking for someone who jumped bail," he said. "That someone has got friends. We are friends of his friends. We would like to convince you to stop looking. We would like to accomplish this without causing you bodily harm, if possible. If not"—he shrugged a fleshy shoulder—"not. Am I getting through to you, Mr. Gunn?"

"Five by five," I said.

"Five by five is military jargon, isn't it? We are not military. We are civilian." He stepped back to take a better look at my Studebaker. "What year?"

"She's a 1950 Starlight coupe."

"Beats me which end is the front end," one of the bouncers said.

"The Studebaker's flat trunk was a distinctive feature," I explained. "What about your Cadillac?" I asked the fedora.

"She's a 1938 LaSalle coupe. The teardrop fenders went out of style after the war. Something like four thousand LaSalles were manufactured, maybe a hundred fifty, two hundred still rolling today."

"Fine-looking automobile," I said.

The short man with the fedora whistled through his teeth. "Your Starlight's no slouch," he said. He removed his hat and mopped his brow on the back of a cuff before carefully setting the hat back on his head, using both hands. "You need to be extra careful driving a vintage car. The last thing you want is to scrape her paint against a fire hydrant."

"It's the last thing," I said.

Nodding as if we'd signed a verbal contract, the short man walked up to the Studebaker and, using the diamond on a pinky ring, scratched the left front fender from end to end. The sound was excruciating.

"Can I assume we understand each other?" he inquired.

"You didn't need to do that," I said. The heel of my right hand was on the molded grip of the Smith & Wesson semiautomatic wedged under my thigh. It could have gone either way.

"I didn't, did I?" he agreed. He tugged down the brim of his fedora to shade his eyes. "Hopefully our paths won't cross again." He took another look at the car and angled his head in admiration. "Some beaut," he said, "scratch notwithstanding."

"You ought to leave me your business card," I said.

"Why would I want to do that?"

"In case I decide to sell the Studebaker."

The four of them exchanged looks. "He's a comedian," one of the bouncers said.

"A regular sit-down comic," the short man in the fedora said.

Jesus Oropesa thought I should be writing movie scripts. These jokers detected a talent for comedy. Good luck in my civilian endeavors.

The four of them backed toward their respective cars, then backed the cars out and headed, with the Cadillac La-Salle leading the way, in the direction of the interstate. I fitted the Smith & Wesson back into the holster attached by a magnet to the underside of the dashboard. It'd been an optional extra when I bought the Studebaker from an L.A. funeral parlor owner going to jail for aiding and abetting. I never asked what he'd been aiding and abetting. He never volunteered the information.

Sixteen

Keeping an eye on the rearview mirror, I drove north, skirting the urban mangle of Albuquerque and the rich-ghetto sprawl of Santa Fe. Taos, an hour and a quarter down the road north of Santa Fe, offers up a different moonscape than the rest of New Mexico. If you don't count the artsy-craftsy crowd and their swank galleries and coffee shops, it still has the feel of a small frontier town, one part Pueblo Indian, one part descendants of frontiersmen who came out in Conestogas chain-smoking stogies to keep the gnats at bay. I passed the Kit Carson house on Kit Carson Road; it'd been turned into a museum celebrating the exploits of the Indian fighter who stood off beyond the range of arrows and shot warriors between the eyes with his Kentucky long rifle, then scalped them to collect the hundred-dollar bounty offered by the territorial government for dead Apaches. What can I say? Frontiers like the American Wild West or the tribal badlands of Afghanistan have been known to turn ordinary folks into ordinary killers.

I had trouble finding the Pueblo youth club, wound up asking directions from an Indian behind the cash register of

one of those twenty-four-hour gas stations. I made it in time
to catch the tail end of the marionette show. In the total
darkness of the club's theater, three puppeteers dressed in
black—Ornella Neppi was one of them—were completely
invisible as they worked the life-sized puppets with sticks.
The illusion was eerily perfect. The puppets seemed so human I was taken aback when I went backstage after the
show and saw them crumpled up in a straw hamper. You
might have jumped to the conclusion they didn't have a bone
in their bodies.

"You could be arrested for puppet slaughter," I told
Ornella.

"There was a time in my life when I couldn't hurt a fly,"
she murmured. "I've moved on," she added in a negatively
charged afterthought. She smiled the barefoot contessa smile,
the one despairingly devoid of joy that I first spotted when
she turned up at the Once in a Blue Moon.

She shut the lid on the straw hamper, imprisoning
the puppets—I was relieved they could breathe through the
straw—and invited me for coffee and doughnuts in the
club's coffeehouse. A song with a drumbeat drowning out
the words was coming from a jukebox. A dozen or so local
adolescents—white boys with crew cuts, Pueblo Indians
with dreadlocks, girls with ears and/or nostrils pierced—sat
on benches around a long table nursing Diet Cokes, which
Friday said was, for reasons unbeknownst to her, the only
kind of Coke they served here. Ornella and I found a table
in the corner the furthest from the jukebox.

"What brings you up to Taos?" she asked.

"You," I said. I blew on my coffee to cool it off (by the time I got around to drinking it, it was cold) as I filled her in on what I'd learned about her bail jumper, Emilio Gava. "Silvio Restivo ring any bells?" I inquired when I'd set out the main points.

She shook her head. I thought I could read puzzlement in her eyes. Yul Brynner would have read it the same way.

"I have some leads to track down in Nevada," I said. "One of them will hopefully take us to Gava's doorstep. All the photographs—at the *Las Cruces Star,* in the police morgue—have disappeared. You saw Gava in court, you posted bail on him. You're the only one I know who knows what he looks like. I need you to come with me to identify him."

She flashed that smile of hers that I was coming to dislike because I didn't know her well enough to know what was behind it. "Of course I'll come with you," she said almost eagerly.

Her puppeteer friends took care of the straw hamper. I led Friday to the Studebaker. Passing in front of it, she spotted the scratch on the fender. "Where'd you get that?" she asked.

"I hit a diamond," I said.

If the answer struck her as curious, she didn't let on. "Beautiful car," she said as she settled into the passenger seat.

"Vintage fifties," I said. "Only thing newfangled are the seat belts. Still has the original radio. If you turn it on all you get is Nat King Cole or Bo Diddley."

She almost but not quite laughed. "I don't even know who Bo Diddley is."

"That's what's called a generation gap," I said. "Chances are you never saw the Ed Sullivan show where Bo Diddley made his national debut."

"I don't know who Ed Sullivan is either."

I mimicked moving closer to her in a wheelchair. "Can you talk louder?" I said. "I have a hearing aid but I can't remember where I put it."

"Hey, you're not that much older than me."

"In my body, maybe fifteen years. In my head, more like twice that."

Working our way down the interstate to the Albuquerque airport neither of us made small talk, but unlike my recent experience with France-Marie the silence never became strained. I parked the Studebaker in the long-term lot as near as I could to the cashier's booth. We took separate rooms in a respectable motel near the terminal. Early morning flights coming in so low they scraped tar off the roof woke us. We checked in for the first plane going in the right direction, a midmorning flight to Flagstaff. Our baggage was carry on—I had my small canvas overnight bag, Friday had her bulky silver astronaut knapsack slung casually over one bare shoulder. She was wearing faded red basketball sneakers without socks, loose-fitting jeans, and that butter-colored sleeveless blouse she'd had on when she came round the mobile home park looking to hire a private investigator. The sleeves of an off-white cardigan tied around her waist hid the sliver of midriff between the blouse and the jeans. The plane had been overbooked. Four people I took for college students and a spry older woman volunteered to leave in exchange for free tickets on a later flight. Friday wasn't even seated next to me—she was on the aisle, across the aisle, three rows up. At the risk of being taken for a spine fetishist, I have to report that I stared at her vertebrae the several times she leaned forward to retrieve something from her knapsack.

I rented an air-conditioned four-wheel-drive Toyota from the Avis people at the Flagstaff airport, ticked the box on the contract to get full insurance, and set out heading west on U.S. 40. We shared a sub at a lunch counter outside of Kingman, then branched off onto Route 68 and crossed the Colorado River above Laughlin, a town booming with flashy casinos and fancy hotels and fleshy roadside billboards advertising same. Seems as if everything for sale these days is being marketed by half-naked ladies. We topped off the gas tank outside of Laughlin, used the facilities, stretched our legs in a picnic area behind the gas station, then set out for Nipton, crossing into California and arriving just after seven. I'd been to Nipton once before—it was when I was towing Once in a Blue Moon from Los Angeles to Hatch—so I pretty much knew what I was getting into. In a previous incarnation it'd been a stagecoach stop between Flagstaff and the coast. Nowadays it consisted of a dozen mobile homes and an equal number of dilapidated buildings, an old-fashioned general store with a potbellied stove inside and a gasoline pump that was "temporarily out of order" outside, and a pleasant enough adobe hotel with four bedrooms and one bathroom in the hallway. Giant hundred-fifty-car Union Pacific freight trains passed a stone's throw from the hotel's porch, rattling the windows, setting the building to trembling on its foundations.

We parked the Toyota under the overhang at the rear of the hotel. A tired cowboy engrossed in a comic book was holding fort behind the check-in counter. He had neglected to take off his Stetson indoors, probably because he felt naked without it. A plastic name tag attached to the flap of the breast pocket of his flannel shirt identified him as Clarence. I had to clear my throat twice to get him to look up from the comic book. He didn't appear to appreciate the interruption. I told Clarence I'd called ahead from the Avis desk in Flagstaff. He moistened a thumb on a postage-stamp sponge and rifled through the pages of a large reservation book until he came to this week's page. He ran a finger down the list, scratching at the names with a fingernail bitten to the quick.

"Only got us four rooms," he remarked.

"That's why I reserved," I said.

"How're we spelling Gun?"

My sidekick answered for me. "With two *n*'s," Friday said.

"I don't got nobody named Gunn on my list. I got a reservation for a Gun with one *n*."

"That's almost certainly me," I said.

He looked up, a frown of disapproval on his face. "Did you go and spell out your name on the phone?"

I said I couldn't remember.

"Well, then, it's sure not our fault if'n it's spelled bad."

"I didn't say it was your fault. What about the two rooms?"

"Only one listed on the reservation." Clarence looked up again with something resembling a lecherous glint in his eye. "Only one still available."

I could see Clarence sizing up the pretty creature standing next to me. She'd put on the cardigan but hadn't bothered buttoning it. I wondered whether he could make out her very spare ribs. I wondered if he was calculating the age difference between her and me.

I looked at Ornella in confusion. "I promise you I asked for—"

"We'll take it," Friday told the night clerk.

"You'll take it?" he asked, looking at me.

"The lady said we'd take it so we'll take it."

I signed the register "Mr. and Mrs. Gun from Hatch." I figured the reservation was in the name of Gun and I didn't want to confound the already confounded cowboy by registering under another name.

Which is how Ornella and I found ourselves sharing a tiny bedroom with a plaque on the door identifying it as the Clara Bow room. Seems as if the legendary silent-screen actress had lived here during the Roaring Twenties when she was building her Shangri-la in the Mojave Desert.

The situation was awkward, to say the least. I can only suppose my desire for Friday was written on my face. Clarence out at the desk certainly spotted it, judging from the way he licked his chapped lips as he slid the room key across the counter. Trouble is I have scruples. The last thing I wanted to do was impose myself on a woman. If something was going to happen in the Clara Bow room, in the Clara Bow double bed, Ornella would have to make the first move.

Which, I am happy to say, is what she did.

Here's what happened. We had supper in the general store. An obliging Chicana named Vesustiana whipped up some hash browns and turkey burgers for us on her two-burner stove. "Where'bouts?" she asked as dished them out right from the frying pan.

"She wants to know where we're from," Ornella explained when she saw the blank look on my face. "We're from Hatch," she told Vesustiana.

"What brings you to Nipton?" she asked.

"We're newlyweds," Friday said with a straight face. "This is our wedding night. For our honeymoon, we're going to explore the Mojave."

"Well, neither of you look like virgins, so I reckon it'll work out real fine. Wedding nights can be bad news for late bloomers who don't have a lot of experience with sexual copulation. Since you're celebrating, coffee's on the house."

Back in the Clara Bow cubbyhole, I asked Ornella why she'd said what she'd said.

She was looking at herself in the small wall mirror with seashells glued to the frame. Suddenly she crossed her arms and took hold of the hem of her shirt and pulled it up and over her head. The sight of her vertebrae left me short of breath.

I could see she was monitoring my reaction in the mirror. "I figured we could beat around the bush, Lemuel. We could laugh nervously at each other's jokes. When I admitted I didn't have the foggiest idea who Clara Bow was, you'd explain at great length. You'd be so edgy you wouldn't economize on words. The subtext of what you said, the message between the lines would be the difference in our ages."

Ornella walked across the narrow room to the window that gave onto the railroad tracks and, beyond that, the Mojave Desert and pulled down the shade. She turned to face me. "How old *are* you, Lemuel?"

"Forty-eight."

"I'm thirty-three. You were smack on when you figured there were fifteen years between us."

She settled cross-legged onto the bed, her spine against the footboard. "There's a Corsican saying my grandfather passed on to me—something about a woman needing to be half her lover's age plus seven if the relationship had a hope in hell of working out. I think the Corsicans got it from the Arabs. So by my Corsican grandfather's rule of thumb, Lemuel, dear, you're much too young for me."

She smiled that patented smile of hers, only this time I thought I detected the faintest suggestion of joy in it. Maybe I was coloring her smile with my own crayons. Maybe I was wishful thinking. Maybe I needed to stop thinking. Her nipples were erect. My luck, both of them were pointing straight at me. This wasn't the moment to play the killjoy.

Without going into details, I can honestly say that I rose to the occasion. At one point I became convinced she was running a fever—until it hit me that the heat coming off her body had another explanation. Her skin was the temperature of the earth I once touched above Dacht-i-Navar, a still active volcano southwest of Kabul in Afghanistan. When I said this out loud, I was rewarded with a ripple of musical laughter, something I couldn't remember hearing from her before. Fact is I could feel myself falling for Friday in a big way—I could feel myself trying to hold myself back and not succeeding. I could see she'd been hurt and hurt badly. The pain was in the smile. The pain was in the back of her eyes. The pain was in the alert, guarded way she had of accepting a lover into her arms. A nasty little voice in the lobe of my brain that houses my early warning system told me hurt people sometimes became addicted to pain—in themselves, in others.

I tuned out the nasty little voice.

In the early hours of the morning one of those endless Union Pacific freight trains rumbled past the hotel. The rattling of the windows, the quaking of the floorboards must have startled Friday because she melted back into my arms as if she were seeking sanctuary. After a long while she whispered in my ear, "You make me hope there is hope."

"Hope is what's left when you pan for gold and come up with pebbles washed smooth in the riverbed."

"Are you always such a wet blanket?"

"I try to keep things in perspective. We can begin to talk about hope when we spend the night in the same bed without making love."

When the freight train's caboose had gone past, the deafening soundlessness of the desert engulfed us. "So I didn't think you'd be a good lover," she said suddenly, her breath warm and moist on my ear. "You took me by surprise."

I pushed her away gently and sat up. "Listen up, Friday. There's no such thing as a good lover or a bad lover. We're different lovers with different people. It's one of the mysteries of life—how one female can turn you into an eager and ardent lover and another can barely get a rise out of you. Go figure."

She sat up alongside me. "Question of chemistry," she said.

"Question of alchemy," I said.

"Panning pebbles in a riverbed and turning them into gold?"

I had to laugh. "That's as good a definition of alchemy as any."

She padded over to the window and raised the shade and came back to the bed. The Clara Bow room was turning shades of gray. The seashells on the small mirror glistened with first light. "Our first sunrise," Friday said. She kissed the shrapnel scar on my right shoulder, then, startled, looked at me. "Where'd you get this?" she whispered.

"Roadside bomb filled with ammonium nitrate—what you call fertilizer—exploded under our Humvee during my first tour in Afghanistan back in 2001. The driver was killed instantly. He was a nineteen-year-old hillbilly who drove me nuts blasting 'Grown Men Don't Cry' on a jury-rigged Blaupunkt. The Afghan officer riding shotgun had both his legs blown off and died of gangrene two days later. I was catnapping in the back so I lucked out—only caught a splinter of shrapnel in the shoulder. Never did find out if the bomb was set by Pashtuns trying to kill Tajiks or Tajiks trying to kill Pashtuns or either, or trying to kill Americans."

Friday pressed her lips to the wound inflicted in the hospital immediately after I was born. And I heard a murmur drift up to me. "We've been lovers for only a third of a day, Lemuel, dear. I'm already sharing your pain."

We made love again. It was one of those drowsily slow, exquisitely sumptuous couplings that only happen in the morning when you're still not a hundred percent awake, when you mistake reality for a dream.

With sunlight flooding the room, I could make out the spume white swell of her breasts and purple welts on one or two of her very spare ribs. She noticed me noticing. "Car accident," she explained. "I was driving my uncle's old Chevy—skidded off the road into a drainage ditch. Seat belt probably saved my hide but left its mark on my rib cage." She smiled sheepishly. "Last thing I expected was to sleep with you so I didn't think you'd ever set eyes on my rib cage."

"I'm tickled pink to wake up to your rib cage," I said. "I'm eager to share *your* pain."

Later on, stuffing ourselves with home-baked raisin muffins in the general store—amazing the appetite you can work up at what Vesustiana called "sexual copulation"—we returned to the business at hand. I retrieved the Sony Walkman from my gear and hit PLAY so we could listen again to the anonymous phone call that sent Detective Awlson off to the Blue Grass to arrest Gava. *"Awright, I have not got all night. What do you say we put this show on the road, huh?"*

We sat there staring at the cassette as if it could provide an image of the speaker if you listened hard enough.

"What can you tell about him from his voice?" she asked.

"He's cocksure of himself, for starters. He knows where the conversation is going because he's steering it. He's shrewd smart as opposed to educated smart. He's probably a poker player who memorized the odds against drawing to an inside straight. He's not someone I'd invite into my Once in a Blue Moon to drink a cold Mexican Modelo. He's not someone I'd tangle with if I could avoid it."

"All that just from his voice?"

"All that and more. I've come across mugs who buy cocaine before."

"I'll bet you have."

Back in the Clara Bow room, Friday suddenly came up with the idea of exchanging tokens to mark the beginning of the beginning. "I told you I was superstitious, remember?" she said. "Here's the thing: We're starting out on a journey together. I need to have something personal of yours, you need to have something personal of mine to make sure we get where we're going in one piece."

I studied her eyes. She was dead serious. I didn't know if the journey in question was the search for her bail jumper or had something to do with what happened in Clara Bow's double bed the night before. Shrugging, figuring I had nothing to lose, I gave her the small piece of shrapnel the Afghan male nurse had pried from my shoulder and I'd used as a fob on my Once in a Blue Moon key chain. She gave me the silver St. Christopher medallion she wore around her neck whenever she was on the road. Turns out her grandfather had given it to her at the airport after her first summer in Corsica. I attached the medal to my key chain. St. Christopher, of course, is the patron saint of voyagers. I wasn't one to put much store in saints but what the heck, it didn't hurt to bet on several horses in any given race.

Seventeen

I'll do Afghanistan now.

I'd been posted to the Company's compound in Kabul, which was Langley's bright idea of R and R after two months in the Pakistani-Afghan badlands. I'd been named acting deputy station chief, which sounds real important until you discover there were eight deputy station chiefs, each one with a bailiwick to preside over. As the station was thick with desk wallahs and thin on officers who'd spent serious time outside the Green Zone, I presided over field operations, which consisted, during my tour in Kabul, of forays into the maze of various medinas in search of Taliban and Hezb-e Islami operatives. Sometimes I'd tag along with the raiders to interrogate suspects myself—I understood enough pidgin Pashto to know when the government translator was leaving out juicy details. Other times I camped in the compound's command bunker to coordinate operations from a distance. I'd sit on a wooden swivel chair, nursing a cold beer, my eyes on the bank of plasma screens showing, among other things, a Wall Street ticker tape, an old episode of *Seinfeld*, and the live feed from minicameras attached to the helmets of soldiers breaking down doors in a medina. I was presiding over one such foray that had reached the operational stage when my station chief—I'll refer to him as Jack for the purposes of this narrative, since the real names of Company employees, mine included, are considered a state secret—suggested I ought to tailgate the Delta-Foxtrot team setting off at midnight to raid a remote village in the rugged ridges of the Hindu Kush in the hope of capturing the especially tall mujahid who'd taught English to Osama bin Laden. (We had the mujahid's photograph on file, it'd been taken from a drone, we calculated his height from the time of day and the length of his shadow.) "If you're on scene, you can begin interrogatin' him from the get-go while he's still disoriented," Jack said. "If you elicit real-time information on the whereabouts of our friend Osama, radio it on in. I'll have another team geared up and airborne in minutes."

The Delta-Foxtrot people had a reputation for being pit bulls—the standing joke held that they could traverse more terrain on foot in a day than run-of-the-mill soldiers could cover in a jeep. Like most exaggerations, it contained a kernel of truth. I wasn't sure I could keep up with them and told Jack as much. "You're goin' to seed sittin' 'round these television screens," he said. "God damn, Lemuel, put on your seven-league hiking boots if you need to but I want your ass out there."

If you've never used night-vision goggles, don't. The feeling of being trapped underwater is so intense you find yourself gasping for air when you first put them on. Two helicopters, flying without lights, deposited us on a flat two ridges downwind from the target, so we had a bit of a slog between us and the village. We scrambled up and down gullies, point gunmen out ahead, followed by the main team, followed by me and my minder, a medical corpsman just back from three weeks of R and R in Japan and sweating bullets under the weight of the rucksack filled with first responder gear. On the downslope of the first ridge I stepped gingerly over the corpse of a young herdsman outside his igloo-shaped stone hut. I could see the hilt of one of those curved Afghan pulwars sticking out of his chest. The goats he'd been guarding, tethered to a long cord stretched taut between the hut and a dead tree, had all had their throats cut. For purposes of the obligatory battle report, I supposed they'd be listed as enemy combatants KIA. We made our way up the second ridge, past a field filled with vines. The grapes hanging from them appeared bluish green through my goggles. I wondered what kind of wine they could make with grapes like that. At the top of the last ridge, the Delta-Foxtrot leader, a baby-faced lieutenant, his face streaked with charcoal, only his eyes clearly visible, dropped to one knee next to me. I thought for a moment he was going to ask me to join him in prayer. "You and Meredith here wait till I radio for you to come on in, hear?" he whispered.

"Hear," I said.

Lying flat on my stomach, my chin on the small radio pack strapped to the folding stock of my M-16, I could make out ghostlike figures, bluish green in their camouflage khakis and flak jackets, swimming downhill toward the drowned village, dark and silent as a sunken ship in a seabed. Somewhere at the edge of the seabed a dog barked, the bark turned into a yelp, the yelp trailed off into a soft whine of pain. I could make out hunched figures running through the alleyways, converging on the mud-walled compound around the whitewashed mosque. Then the first shots echoed through the village—bloated blasts from the old smooth-bored rifles the mujahideen had used in their ten-year jihad against the Russians, falsetto bursts from the automatic weapons of our raiders. A grenade—one of those fragmentation thingamabobs with a fifteen-meter kill radius—exploded next to the massive wooden door of the mosque compound, blowing it off its hinges. A geyser of smoke and dust rose from the seabed.

"So much for surprising them," I whispered to Meredith.

Inside the mosque compound, a woman screamed in Pashto—I understood that she wanted a girl or several girls to run to the mosque. An especially tall man in a bluish green djellaba materialized in a doorway and fired his rifle into the head of a raider at point-blank range. Spinning, he tried to shoot again. The rifle must have jammed, because he took hold of the barrel and began to use it as a club, swinging wildly at the bluish green figures in camouflage khaki swarming around him. The terrified shrieks of young girls pierced the night.

"I'm going in," I told Meredith.

"Lieutenant said we was to wait till he radioed up to us," he said.

"Lieutenant may be otherwise occupied," I said. I pushed

myself to my feet, flicked off the safety on my M-16, and started downhill through ankle-high underbrush that undulated like seaweed as I waded through it. I could hear Meredith, out of breath from an overdose of adrenaline, sliding, slipping, scampering downslope behind me. At the edge of the village I came across the first corpses, two Afghans, one a boy, one a grandfather judging from his long bluish green beard, sprawled on the ground next to a dead dog. All three were bleeding bright orange blood from slit throats. There were other corpses, maybe a dozen, maybe more, I stopped counting at eight. In the mosque compound, the corpse of the dead American who'd been shot at point-blank range was being zipped into a black canvas body bag, his dog tags wired to one of the plastic grips. Two raiders had literally pinned the especially tall man to the mud wall with bayonets thrust through the cloth of his bluish green djellaba. The left side of his face was vivid purple, bright orange blood oozed from an open wound under his left eye. Unintelligible words rose from his throat. If this was bin Laden's English teacher, he would need an extended sick leave before he taught anyone anything again.

"Go ahead and interrogate the bastard," the lieutenant said.

I approached the prisoner. "What's your name?" I asked.

Our Afghan translator repeated my question in Pashto.

The mujahid stared at me with his one eye that was still operational—I couldn't tell, even with my night-vision goggles, if the other eye was shut or no longer existed. "Fuck America," he whispered in English. "Fuck George Bush."

One of the soldiers pinning him to the mud wall was wearing fingerless biker's gloves. Still holding the handle of the bayonet with his left hand, he reared back with his right and punched the prisoner in the groin.

The mujahid doubled over and coughed up crimson bile. Straightening with an effort, he spat out, in English, "Fuck your mother."

"He don't learn from his mistakes," the soldier wearing biker's gloves remarked.

Terrible shrieks came from the mosque. I turned to see raiders dragging two teenage girls and an older woman by their long hair over the rocky ground to the middle of the compound. All three females had been stripped naked. Seen through my goggles, their pale skin appeared bluish green.

"You need to stop this," someone said. I turned back to see who had spoken. The lieutenant and his Delta-Foxtrot people were all staring at me.

One of the soldiers nodded in my direction. "He say sumptin?" he asked.

"You say something?" the lieutenant inquired.

"The herdsman on the hill, his goats were probably enemy combatants," I said. "These woman aren't." My words were devoid of consonants, as if they originated with a ventriloquist not moving his lips when he threw his voice.

"Fucking mujahid went and killed one of my men," the lieutenant said, as if that explained everything. "His wife, his kids, they have got to pay the blood price. That's the only language these Taliban shits understand."

An inhuman groan came from the mujahid—I thought

at first he was trying to clear blood from the back of his throat until I noticed his one eye staring past me at his wife and daughters, who were being sodomized by the dark figures in camouflage khakis. Two of them had their pants down around their ankles, their bare asses burning bluish green in the riptide of this awful night. Funny thing is how, when I picture the scene, when I remember the unspeakable things they were doing to the woman and the two girls, in my mind's eye I see it all happening in a kind of sluggish sea-swell slow motion.

"I'm going to report what I saw here," I announced.

"What the fuck did he see here?" one of the soldiers pinning the especially tall mujahid to the wall demanded.

"Me, I didn't see nuttin' out of the usual," a second soldier said.

Three sharp shots sounded behind me. I am ashamed to say I was afraid to turn and look—afraid of what I would see, afraid of what I would do if I saw.

"Killed resisting arrestation," one of the soldiers snickered. "Ain't that a fact, John Henry?"

"Teach 'em to resist arrestation," John Henry agreed.

"Lieutenant, what d'we do wit the prisoner?"

"You're supposed to take him back for interrogation," I said.

The only eye available to the especially tall mujahid fixed me with a look of infinite grief. And the baby-faced lieutenant who presided over the absence of civilization in this Hindu Kush seabed reached out with the tippy-tip of the barrel of his M-16 and gently wedged it, like a dentist probing for a loose tooth, into the mujahid's mouth. "Stand away," the lieutenant snapped. The two soldiers pinning the mujahid to the wall stepped back smartly. Gagging on the rifle barrel in his mouth, the especially tall mujahid, held up by the two bayonets pinning him to the wall, wilted into his bluish green djellaba.

"Don't do that—" I heard myself groan, but he did do that, he angled the barrel so that it was pointing toward the endless expanse of universe over our heads and he pulled the trigger. The mujahid's skull exploded, splattering brain matter on all the bluish green uniforms within a fifteen-meter stain radius.

The withdrawal from the village passed in an adrenaline haze—rotors beating the air, stirring up gravel and dust and debris, two helicopters touching down on the perimeter of the seabed, gunships hovering overhead stabbing the alley-ways and the mosque compound with shards of brilliant bluish green light. Bodies were gathered and piled like so much deadwood. As I lumbered across a field, I nearly stumbled over the figure of a crouched girl. I was afraid she might be wounded and tugged her to her feet looking for blood. She was skinny and dirty and scared out of her skull but not bloodstained. I remember thinking she must have been around twelve but discovered later she was an undernourished, overfrightened fifteen. I pulled her toward the nearest helicopter and, gripping her under the armpits, hefted her into it. Sitting on the metal floor, she stared at me with unblinking eyes. The helicopter door slammed shut. Nobody complained about a passenger. "I'm Gunn," I called over the whirring rotors, tapping my chest. When she didn't say anything I pointed at her. "You?" The Afghan translator sitting across from us shouted to her in Pashto. She turned back to me. "Kubra," she said. "Kubra," I nodded. As the helicopter lifted off, there was an enormous explosion in the village behind me. It lit up the night sky visible through the oval Plexiglas windows, transforming the other hovering helicopter into a night moth.

When I got back to Kabul base, I parked the girl in the station infirmary and woke my station chief. "Jack," I said, "bad things happened out there tonight."

He was sitting in his skivvy shorts on a steel cot. His mane of hair, once dirty blond, now dirty gray, was disheveled. He threaded his fingers through it several times working out knots. I noticed several empty whisky bottles on the cement floor under the cot. "How would you know what happened out there tonight?" he asked.

"You told me to tailgate the raid."

"You have that in writing?" he demanded. "You're supposed to be in the command bunker during a raid."

"I was out there with Delta-Foxtrot," I said. "I saw them drag naked females across the compound. They killed the females—"

"You saw them kill these females?"

"I heard the shots. There were three females. There were three shots."

"You saw the bodies?"

I concentrated on Jack's bare feet, which he was fitting into ornate Afghan slippers

"You didn't actually see bodies, huh, Lemuel?"

"I didn't see *those* bodies . . . I was too frightened to turn around and look." I sucked the stale air of the bedroom into my lungs. It struck me that the stale air of a station chief's bunkroom could be more harmful than cigarette smoke. I could hear sirens wailing somewhere in the city but I could never tell from the pitch whether they were fire engines or ambulances or police cars escorting VIPs in and out of the Green Zone. "I saw the lieutenant murder the especially tall mujahid," I said. "The stain on my shirt—it's his brains, Jack."

"Lemuel, Lemuel, he was an enemy combatant. Delta-Foxtrot lost one of their men in the raid. They radioed in he was shot in the head by your especially tall mujahid. You know standin' operational procedure as well as me—we take Taliban alive when we can, we leave them dead when we can't."

I murmured something about needing to file a report.

"File, file. This war is a quagmire. One more report in triplicate won't keep us from sinking in deeper."

It took me hours to write out what I wanted to write out. I preempted the screen showing the *Seinfeld* rerun and typed it up with one finger, then I rewrote it (you'll laugh) leaving out all the consonants from my own dialogue, then I re-rewrote it putting them back in because words without consonants come across as gibberish. I wound up, in the umpteenth version, pretty much telling the story as I've set it out here. I printed out three copies and put my John Hancock on the last page and dispatched the report on up the chain of command. Jack, which, you may remember, wasn't his real name, put his initials on the top right and sent it on up, through channels, to the Company's in-country commander, who sent it on up, through channels, to the Afghan desk in D.C. All this took time. Lots of time. I lost track of what happened after my report reached Washington as the senior brass who may or may not have read it weren't required to initial the single copy that made its way back downhill to me stamped NOT ACTIONABLE. It seems the baby-faced lieutenant and his Delta-Foxtrot people had been rotated out of Afghanistan. It seems the target village in the Hindu Kush had been abandoned by the Afghans who survived the raid. It seems their empty mud huts had been used by army demolition specialists to teach greenhorns how to blow up what passed for a house in this godforsaken wasteland of a country. I still had two months, two days left on my Kabul tour (like Millie Kugler's husband, Hank, I would mark off the days on a calendar) when the classified cable firing me for reasons deemed too secret to spell out reached my desk. I was already opening beer bottles with my thumb and index finger and crushing the metal tops between my fingers. The Company, which obviously didn't appreciate whistle-blowers, neglected to add the usual war zone bonus to my termination check. (When I raised the matter with the disbursing officer, he shut his eyes tiredly. "Go sue us," he said.) Whatever pension credits I had were out the window. A form letter from the station chief was paper-clipped to the cable. It thanked me for unspecified services to my country and wished me good luck in my civilian endeavors.

Good luck in my civilian endeavors! Screw him.

Jack's real name, the one on the bottom of his insulting letter, was Jack F. for Francis Coburn. Jack ass.

Go sue me for revealing a state secret. It'll give me a chance to tell what happened on the Hindu Kush in open court.

You wanted to know where my anger comes from. It comes from my gut.

Eighteen

According to this Clark County Historical Society brochure I came across on a shelf in the Nipton general store, Searchlight got its name when a miner tunneling into a hill lit a Searchlight brand match on the sole of his boot and caught sight of a vein of gold. That was back before the turn of the last century. Searchlight, astride the old Arrowhead Highway, boomed until the twenties when the vein began to run dry and U.S. 91 swung around the town instead of through it. The gold diggers drifted away to mine other veins: in Reno, Nevada, for instance. Leaving five hundred or so people clinging to a bygone era by their fingernails.

We were Searchlight bound in the rental Toyota. Ornella Neppi was driving, *"All my exes live in Texas, that's why I hang my hat in Tennessee"* was playing on the car radio, I was stretched out in the back trying to catch up on the shut-eye I'd missed out on the night before. "Will you take a look at *this*!" Friday exclaimed as she braked the car onto the gravel shoulder. I sat up so quickly I banged my head against the roof of the car. Ornella was peering through the front window at a historical marker indicating the direction to Walking Box Ranch, Clara Bow's Shangri-la after her Nipton interlude. "It might be worth the detour," she said as I scrambled past the stick shift onto the front seat. Her tone was mischievous. "I mean, I *am* a great Clara Bow fan. I'm seriously considering starting a Clara Bow fan club in Doña Ana. Thanks to you, I know who she is. And I know what can happen when someone sleeps in her bed. Come on, spoilsport. It's only seven miles into the Mojave. What do we have to lose?"

"Time," I said. "We need to concentrate on Searchlight if we're going to pick up the trail of your Emilio Gava."

A dark cloud discolored the seaweed green in her eyes. "Why is he suddenly *my* Emilio Gava?"

"He's your Emilio Gava in the sense that it's you who posted the bail he's jumping."

She took several deep breaths, which naturally drew my attention to her chest. As usual I wasn't looking for campaign ribbons. "Want me to drive?" I asked.

"Sure."

I walked around the Toyota and got in behind the wheel, pushing the lever to push the seat back. She slid across to the passenger side. I drove past the small airport on into town and pulled up in front of the only place that looked open for business, one of those old-fashioned hardware stores with aisle upon aisle of wooden shelving and dim electric lighting. MILLMAN & SON HARD AND SOFT WARE was written in fresh gold lettering above the door. There was a collection of barbed wire in a frame on a wall, samples of the different "bobbed wire" used by cattlemen to fence off grazing land in the Texas Panhandle. The name of each sample was printed underneath it: the Crandal Zigzag, the Merrill Buffalo, the Allis Sawtooth, Upham's Snail.

"You interested in barb wire?" an elderly gentleman with silky gray whiskers inquired from the back of the store.

"Not especially," I said.

He ambled down one of his aisles toward us. "I'm the Millman of Millman & Son. Son's gone up to Carson City to check out a radio-controlled model plane fair. Max-Leo, that's the son in Millman & Son, he's the one that went and added the software to my hardware—he has got hisself a line of computer software, hi-tech, low-tech, no-tech gizmos, microphones, recording devices, video cameras, he has got RAM and ROM and VDU and VDT, damned if I know what they all mean but Max-Leo sells them and repairs them. Seems like as if he's gonna add radio-controlled model aeroplanes. Where Max-Leo will end only God knows and he ain't confiding in your servant."

Ornella picked a pair of goggles off a shelf. "I could never bring myself to open my eyes underwater," she said.

"Them there ain't underwater goggles, miss."

"They're army PVS-7 night-vision goggles," I said. "If there's starlight or a slice of moon, you can see as if it's day-time except everything you see looks greenish."

"How do you know all that?" Ornella asked.

"There're parts of me you haven't been to yet," I said.

"How much?" Ornella asked Mr. Millman.

"Brand new, they go for $2,699. These here are third-hand. Max-Leo went and retooled them back to factory condition. They'll set you back"—he scratched at a whisker—"three hundred, the case, the head strap, two AA batteries thrown in."

"Two fifty," Ornella said.

"Two seventy-five is my last price. You can take it or you can not take it, all the same to me."

"You accept credit cards?"

"I accept checks on the barrelhead long as you got ID."

"What are you planning to do with night-vision goggles?" I asked Ornella as she wrote out a check on the top of a barrel.

"I always wanted to see what's going on around me at night. Now's my chance."

I turned back to Mr. Millman. "We're looking for the Original Searchlight Speakeasy Saloon."

"Well, now, you ain't gonna find the Original Searchlight Speakeasy Saloon, are you? For the simple reason it don't exist no more. Went out of business two, two and a half years ago when the tourist trade trickled off. They had themselves a giant-screen TV. Fact is, everybody's got a giant-screen TV if you sit close enough to it, but that's another story. Saloon turned into a guesthouse upstairs, Mojave Medical Supply downstairs, a unisex beauty parlor in the basement. Hell, I never yet met no one who was unisex, but then I ain't said my last word, have I? Beauty parlor still goes by the name of Speakeasy. Speakeasy Beauty Emporium. The beauty parlor finished up with the saloon's name and the saloon's giant TV. Bunch of us go down there Monday nights to get our hair cut and watch football. Need any of those things—bed and breakfast at the guesthouse, crutches, oxygen bottle, wheelchair, haircut, *Monday Night Football*—I can direct you to the location."

Friday avoided my eye. "Does the guesthouse have a Clara Bow room by any chance?"

"I'll require mouth-to-mouth resuscitation if I cross the threshold of one more Clara Bow room," I told Mr. Millman.

"Hey, I do mouth-to-mouth, Lemuel dear. Just say the word."

"Damnation, you people talking English or what?" Millman of Millman & Son asked.

Ornella Neppi lowered her eyes and smiled. "We've got a secret language," she confessed.

I was starting to be comfortable with Friday's smile. Even when she directed it at someone else, I had the feeling it was meant for me. Maybe that's what she had in mind when she decided we needed to exchange tokens to mark the beginning of the beginning. "I'd take it kindly if you would point us toward the former Speakeasy Saloon," I told Mr. Millman.

"No problem," he said. He pushed open the screen door and stepped onto the porch to give us directions. "Drive on down to that stop sign over there. You be sure to come to a full stop 'cause Furman, he's part-time sheriff, part-time undertaker, sometimes hangs out in an alleyway to ticket offenders. You'll be forty bucks lighter if he nabs you. Okay, you turn right at the stop, you go on down Cottonwood Cover Road past Furman's police station, you can't miss it because his police car, which is broken, is up on cinder blocks in front of it, you drive on down—what?—I reckon a mile would be 'bout right. Long 'bout where Searchlight ends and them hills out yonder begin you'll see a three-story frame building, that there's the Speakeasy. You can't miss it, it's directly across from the Mojave Mobile Home Park."

We followed Hillman's directions and found the three-story onetime saloon on the edge of town. It still had faded but readable lettering across the frontage that said THE ORIGINAL SEARCHLIGHT SPEAKEASY SALOON. A small billboard in the yard, the kind planted in front of churches, listed the businesses on the premises. Searchlight Guest House. Mojave Medical Equipment. The Speakeasy Beauty Emporium. I pulled around to the side of the building and parked in the shade.

"So you're the detective," Friday said. "What do we do now?"

"Not sure," I said. We were standing at the corner of the building and I was staring at the sign in the front yard. "Speakeasy Beauty Emporium," I said, thinking out loud. "Why'd they keep the Speakeasy logo? If they kept the Speakeasy logo, maybe they kept the . . ." I turned to Ornella. "You don't happen to have a portable telephone in that silver astronaut sack of yours?" She nodded yes and, reaching into the front pocket, produced it. "First time I get to use one of these contraptions," I said. I pecked out Detective Awlson's number with a fingernail because the numbers on the phone were too small for my fingertips. When he picked up I said, "Listen up, Detective, I'm in Searchlight looking for Gava's girlfriend name of Annabel. Can you read me off that phone number Gava called from Hattie Hillslip's kitchen phone?"

I copied it onto my pad, cut the connection and began dialing the number Awlson had given me.

"Who're you calling?" Ornella asked.

"Whoever answers is who I'm calling," I said. I could hear a telephone purring on the other end. A woman came on the line. I held the earpiece away from my ear so Friday could catch the conversation. "Speakeasy Beauty Emporium," the woman said. "Sharon speaking. You calling for a booking?"

Friday took the phone. "My husband and I are passing through Searchlight. We saw your sign. Would it be possible to come by now?"

"Sure you can, honey, long as you don't mind reading fashion magazines for ten, fifteen minutes."

I trailed after Friday into the building, down a narrow staircase and through a swinging door into what was once the basement of the Original Searchlight Speakeasy Saloon. The Beauty Emporium consisted of a large space that stank of chemicals I couldn't identify—I supposed the unpleasant odor came from products used to dress hair, which is one reason I never went in for hair dressing. You couldn't miss the fact that the parlor was underground—narrow horizontal windows set high in the walls gave onto street level. I caught a glimpse of bicycle wheels passing by. Long neon tubes, one of them sizzling and blinking, hung overhead. A large framed portrait of Jesus filled most of the back brick wall, a small framed photograph of Ronald Reagan hung on another wall above the giant TV, a printed price list was thumbtacked to the back of the door. An older woman and a teenage girl were sitting under giant helmetlike hair dryers, thumbing through L.L.Bean catalogs. The noise from the dryers made conversation difficult.

"You must be Sharon," I called to the proprietor, a badly bleached middle-aged blonde wearing what I took to be a faded Indian sari with its embarrassingly bare midriff. She drifted away from her customers and approached me until her face was inches away from mine. When she angled her head inquisitively, I said, "My name's Gunn. I'm a private investigator." I flipped open my wallet to give her a looksee at my laminated New Mexico ID. "I'm trying to locate someone who worked at the Original Searchlight Speakeasy Saloon."

Sharon eyed Friday. "So you're not here to get your hair styled?"

Ornella shook her head. Sharon turned back to me. "The Speakeasy Saloon gave up the ghost two years ago come summer."

"I see you inherited the Speakeasy logo," I said.

"Had to if I wanted to inherit the Speakeasy phone number."

"Why'd you want the Speakeasy phone number?"

"It was either that or wait ten months for the phone people to get around to running me in a new line with a new number. 'Tain't easy launching a beauty emporium without a telephone. I'm still listed in the phone book as the Original Searchlight Speakeasy Saloon but everyone in Searchlight knows I'm the Emporium so, heck, I figure why bother changing it. Oh, I still get calls now and then from folks trying to reserve a table near the big-screen TV so I know right off they're not calling to get their hair styled. I bought the TV off the saloon when it shut down but I only turn it on Monday nights for the gentlemen who come around to watch football."

"Did you by any chance know an Annabel who worked at the saloon?"

"Oh my gosh, yes. Annabel was one of the three girls who waited tables. To my mind she was a mite too friendly with the customers—waiting tables, you need to keep a respectable distance between you and the clients, specially the male of the species who are all touchy-feely. She had a boyfriend that I never set eyes on. He must've roughed her up some—there were days when she came in wearing a lot of eye makeup and a scarf around her neck. Different folks, different strokes is what I always say. I talked Annabel into going to church, I think it helped her deal with whatever she was dealing with. When the saloon shut down, the other two girls moved on but Annabel was local so I took her in here. I taught her to wash and brush. Of course, I do all the actual cutting and styling."

"Did she get personal calls during work hours?"

"From time to time."

"Was the caller a man?"

Sharon nodded carefully. "It was a man, all right. I usually answer the phone in the Emporium so I heard the voice on the other end. I think it might have been the boyfriend that roughed her up because Annabel didn't look none too happy speaking to him."

"Did you by chance overhear any of these conversations?"

"It's not my habit to listen in on someone else's conversation. Besides which, Annabel always walked over to the far corner and turned her back when she talked on the phone."

"Would you know where I can find her?"

Sharon pursed her lips in indecision. "Sunday and today are her days off," she said. "Don't know as she'd take kindly me giving out her whereabouts."

Friday stepped into the breach. "We're not going to hassle her," she told Sharon. "We just want to talk to her about the man who called her here."

"He in some kind of trouble?"

"He got himself arrested in New Mexico for buying drugs," I said. "We got hold of his phone records. We thought, from the records, he was calling the Speakeasy Saloon. All the time he was calling the Speakeasy Beauty Parlor—"

"Emporium," Sharon said. "It's a beauty emporium."

"Sorry. The Speakeasy Beauty Emporium. A neighbor of his who overheard his end of a conversation thought he mentioned someone named Annabel. That's how come we came by."

Friday said, "The man who was arrested may be thinking of jumping bail. Annabel may know where he is. Save him a lot of grief if we can find him and convince him not to jump."

"Heck, I just plain don't know—"

I stretched the truth to get at the truth. "If we don't talk to Annabel, the police will."

The teenage girl under one of the dryers reached down and tugged the electric plug out of the wall. Half the noise in the Emporium died away. "I think I'm finished, Sharon," the girl called over. She ducked out from under the helmet and, leaning forward to see herself in the mirror, ran both her hands through her newly curled hair to fluff it up.

Sharon shrugged in resignation. "Annabel lives in one of them mobile homes cross the road," she said.

"You know her family name?" I asked.

"Annabel's Annabel Saxby. Her great-granddaddy was one of the original Searchlight gold rush Saxbys. Saxby's a name that rings bells here." Suddenly Sharon reached for Friday's hand. "Do you accept Jesus Christ as your lord and savior?" she demanded.

Her question broke over our conversation with the intensity of a rainsquall. Ornella looked at me in confusion—confusion is the wrong word, alarm would be more accurate—before turning back to Sharon. "No, I don't, actually."

Sharon smiled sadly. "Well, if I was in your shoes, this is something I'd worry my pretty head about. Jesus can't make you win the lottery if you don't buy a ticket. Come home to Jesus when you can, dear."

The teenage girl was putting the L.L.Bean catalog back on the pile on the shelf. She obviously overheard the exchange between Friday and Sharon. "I went and came home to Jesus," she told Ornella. "I'm here to bear witness he saves them that repents the error of their ways. How much I owe you, Sharon?"

"The usual, Cathy-Jo."

Strange as this sounds, Ornella seemed to be fighting back tears when we reached the street. "You okay?" I asked.

She wasn't okay. She settled onto one of the Speakeasy's wooden steps, a point of pain in her eyes. "When I spent summers in Corsica, my grandfather would take me to church with him on Sundays," she said. Her voice fell to a whisper and I had to crouch down to hear her. "I was maybe eight or nine, so everything seemed larger than it probably was. The church swallowed me like a cathedral, a giant Jesus hung crucified on an enormous cross, a great big tear was running down the marble cheek of an enormous Virgin. Then, one Sunday . . ."

Ornella leaned forward and rested her forehead on her knees as if she felt faint and was trying to get the blood flowing to her brain again. "One Sunday what?" I said.

She straightened up slowly. "One Sunday my grandfather stopped going to church. When I asked him why, he said he'd had to kill someone and couldn't look Jesus in the eye again. He said it'd been a matter of family honor."

"Did you ever find out who he killed?"

Breathing deeply, Ornella looked away, her eyes fixed on a horizon that existed only in her mind's eye. "The subject never came up again. Sharon's 'Come home to Jesus when you can' made me think of my grandfather who couldn't come home to Jesus." Suddenly she focused on me. "Did you kill anyone in Afghanistan, Lemuel?"

"Is there a difference between killing someone and letting someone be killed?"

"I don't know. I need to think about it."

I tried to remember what I'd seen on the Hindu Kush. "Me, too, I need to think about it." I stood up. "At least you don't have the same problem as your grandfather. *You* haven't killed anyone."

Then Ornella Neppi said something so softly it sounded like she was talking to herself. "Not yet."

Not yet?

An eighteen-wheeler ripped past us heading for the Mojave hills. For some reason the driver, who was wearing a striped railroad cap, reached up over his head and pulled the horn cord, and a long loud blast startled the birds on the roof of the Speakeasy Saloon into the air. Across the street people popped out of their mobile homes to see what the fuss was. But the fuss had already vanished in a cloud of dust.

Nineteen

Annabel Saxby lived in a small one-room aluminum mobile home, three rows down and four trailers in across the street from Sharon's beauty parlor. There was a tiny garden with a knee-high picket fence on either side of the front door. Wilted geraniums filled the flower beds. "You need to water more," I told the woman who, responding to my knock, opened the door.

"They charge an arm and a leg for water here," she said. "Sharon called to say you was on your way over. She didn't name your name."

"It's Gunn." I could hear what sounded like a television quiz program coming from inside her mobile home. "Lemuel Gunn," I said.

"With two *n*'s," Ornella added playfully. "He's very uptight about people spelling his name right. I'm Ornella Neppi with two *p*'s. I don't care how people spell my name."

"Sharon said you was a detective," Annabel said.

I nodded. "Can we talk to you for a minute?"

Annabel Saxby was in her late twenties and a fine-looking female with very bad taste in clothing: skintight jeans that must have stopped blood from circulating below her ankles, open-toed high-heeled shoes, shocking pink toenails, a tacky blouse unbuttoned down to a washed-out brassiere. She had streaked the hair that she dislodged from her mascara-heavy eyelids with a toss of her head so abrupt it set her earrings, modeled on minichandeliers, to tinkling. She glanced from me to Friday and back to me. "If you come around 'bout Silvio—"

I filled in the blanks so she would think we knew more than we did. "Silvio Restivo. Nicknamed 'the Wrestler.' He dropped from sight eight months ago after he turned state's evidence against Salvatore Baldini. We understand you've been in touch with him off and on since."

"Where'd you get that notion?"

"Phone records. He called you at the Speakeasy beauty parlor nine times in eight months. You called him at his East of Eden condominium once. He got angry at you for calling him there, remember?"

"Silvio and me, we may have talked now and then," Annabel allowed. "Was that a crime?" She chewed on the inside of a cheek. "Sharon said you said he'd been busted for doing dope."

"Buying, not doing," I said. "Cocaine, to be exact. Was he doing drugs when you hung out with him?"

"A little recreational hit now and then, nothing to write home about."

"Is that what made him violent?" Ornella asked.

Annabel was suddenly wide alert. "What makes you think he was violent?"

"It's nothing to be ashamed of," Ornella said softly. "It's not your fault if—"

"Who the hell you people think you are, turning up here uninvited, telling me I got nothing to be ashamed of 'cause of how Silvio got his kicks. Holy shit, I'm not ashamed a nothing!" She turned to go, then spun back so abruptly her chandelier earrings rattled. "Is that what Sharon told you? That Silvio beat up on me?"

I tried to change the subject. "When Silvio phoned you at the beauty parlor—"

"It's a beauty emporium," Annabel said irritably. "A emporium's different from a parlor."

"Emporium, right. When he called you, did you know where he was calling from?"

"He coulda been calling from the moon for all I know." She sat down heavily on her top step. "He never told me where he was and I never asked him, which is how come I never knew."

"You called his home at least once—you must have recognized New Mexico's 505 area code when you dialed the number."

"There was something Mario said needed passing on right away. Silvio left me a number for emergencies. I dialed it once. All I knew was that 505 was out of state but I didn't know which state it was out of state in. Silvio wasn't thrilled with me calling him where he lived—he told me I reached him at a bad time. Sounded as if he had a house full of people."

"What was the message that was so important you used Silvio's emergency number?"

"I wouldn't have called it a message. It was more like a single word."

"What word?"

"Whistlestop."

"Mario wanted you to pass the word 'whistlestop' on to Silvio?"

"Whistlestop, yeah. I don't even know if that's a thing or a place or a password or the code name for a local hooker or what."

"What did Silvio say when you passed on 'whistlestop'?"

"He said to tell Mario he got the message."

I gestured for Ornella to back off a bit and sat down next to Annabel, hoping she would relate more to men who were old enough to be her father. "Were you and Silvio still seeing each other? Were you still his girlfriend? Is that why he kept in touch with you?"

"How could I be seeing someone who was hiding out in an out-of-state area code?"

"You knew he was hiding?"

"Lookit, I'm not as innocent as I look. I *guessed* he was hiding out. He'd need to be pretty dumb not to be hiding out after Salvatore Baldini caught a bullet in the eye."

"So if you weren't seeing each other—weren't still dating, that's what I'm getting at—why all those phone calls?"

Annabel couldn't believe how slow I was. "He called *me* 'cause he didn't want to call the casino," she said in exasperation. "I was, like, the middleman. He called me, I called Mario over at the casino and passed on Silvio's questions. Then I'd pass on Mario's answer next time Silvio called."

"What kind of messages was Mario sending to Silvio, Annabel?"

"Am I gonna be in hot water for passing on messages?"

"You're better off coming clean with me. If you wind up talking to the police, you'll probably need a lawyer."

I let this sink in. Annabel did, too. Finally she came clean. "They was numbers mostly. Mario made me write them down and read them back so I wouldn't get them screwed up."

I jumped to a conclusion. "Bank account numbers."

She tossed the hair out of her eyes. "Bank account numbers, Swift code numbers insteada bank names. Silvio had me pegged for a dumb broad. It never entered his thick head I could figure out what he was doing."

"But you did?"

"Fucking-A I did. Everyone who knew Silvio, everyone in the casino crowd up in Clinch Corners, figured he was being paid off by Mario and the Ruggeris for setting up Salvatore Baldini."

"What was in it for you, being Silvio's middleman?"

"I'd get a envelope stuffed with brand-new twenties in my post box at the post office each time Silvio calls me and I call Mario or vice versa."

"Did you ever meet this Mario?"

"Silvio brought him around once or twice when the Speakeasy was still a saloon and I was waitressing there, that's before it became a emporium and Sharon turned me into a hair stylist. He was hot to trot, Silvio—he wanted to rope me into a"—Annabel glanced quickly at Ornella Neppi—"he tried to rope me into a threesome. He wanted to watch me do it with Mario while he was doing it with me. I said thanks but no thanks, twosomes is my personal private limit, 'specially with Silvio needing to work out his not a hundred percent kosher fantasies. Don't get me wrong. Silvio may a roughed me up some but he was a pussy cat before and after. He's the one that gave me these earrings." She shook her head to make them tinkle.

Ornella, subdued, said, "They're very pretty."

"So are yours," Annabel said.

Ornella smiled at her. "Thanks."

"What does this Mario look like?" I asked.

"He's on the short side, short and thickset."

I took a shot in the dark. "He wears a fedora and round eyeglasses that are thick as windowpanes."

"You know Mario!" Annabel exclaimed in surprise.

"How do you know Mario?" Ornella asked.

"Our lifelines intersected. I got a bone to pick with him. Son of a gun scratched my car."

Twenty

I'll never get the hang of these mobile thingamabobs—
they're so darn small I'm worried I'll wind up with one
lodged like a bone in my throat if I talk into it. I'd need a
Heimlich to expel it so I could breathe again. Explain to me,
for Pete's sake, how a device that fits into your fist can have
someone's entire address book inside. I rate mobile telephones
right up there with plastic credit cards as toxic waste. Public
phone booths, even ones that'd been used as toilets, have always been good enough for me. Trouble is there aren't that
many of them around these days. We were five miles out of
Searchlight on our way down to Clinch Corners and we
hadn't passed a one. Well, I'm exaggerating. We passed one
near the Searchlight airport but the phone box had been
pried off the back wall of the booth and cannibalized. We
passed another at the edge of town but all that was left of
that booth was the cement foundation and some dangling
phone cables. I was driving at the time and seeing the
booths reminded me I'd forgotten to check in with my lady
accountant from the telephone in the Nipton general store.
I'd been hung over from the previous night, I suppose,

though it wasn't alcohol that had stupefied me. Passing a third booth that looked as if it had been in a head-on collision with a truck I gave up and asked Ornella if I could use her contraption. She dialed France-Marie's number in Las Cruces and held the phone over to my ear. I could hear France-Marie saying, "Leave a message if you must," so I understood I'd reached that infernal machine that answers for her when she's not home. "France-Marie," I shouted.

"You don't need to yell like that," Ornella said. "Talk in your everyday voice, okay?"

"France-Marie," I said, "if you hear this, here's a phone number you can pass on to Kubra if she needs to get hold of me in a hurry." I read off the number of the Nipton Hotel on the calling card I'd pocketed at breakfast that morning. "I guess that's it. I'm going to hang up now. Uh, I almost forgot, it's me, Gunn. Okay? Okay, bye."

The Sierra Nevadas in the distance reminded me of mountain ranges in Afghanistan near the Pakistan border—could be all mountain ranges resembled each other when the day wanes and the murkiness rises off the ground like smog. Ornella dozed in the front seat until I rounded a curve a bit too fast and startled her awake. Shaking her head to clear it, she retrieved her mobile again and called her uncle over in Doña Ana to fill him in on where we were at with the bail jumper.

Where we were at had a strong resemblance to a dead end.

The lights were coming on as we rolled into Clinch Corners, a man-made township a couple of hundred yards inside Nevada on the Nevada-California state line. Location, as they say in the gag trade, is everything. This was surely true for Clinch Corners. Witness the endless stream of headlights coming from the direction of Los Angeles. I think there may have been a Pony Express relay stable here once, I think it was a Mr. Clinch, Christian name lost to posterity, who gave his name to it. By the time the two Italian families decided to put down roots here, one on either side of the four-lane highway that stretched from Los Angeles to Las Vegas, Clinch was nothing more than a historical note on a brittle page of an old *Farmers' Almanac*.

The roots, of course, sprouted into two gaudy casinos. By the time we pulled into town, both were lit up like passenger liners at sea, not that I've ever seen passenger liners at sea. Comparison number two: The casinos were lit up like the perimeter of the Green Zone in Kabul after lockdown. That I have seen. Besides the casinos, the township consisted of a gas station and fifty or so mobile homes parked among Joshua trees in the field behind the gas station. Ornella and I found a Pullman car that had been transformed into a diner at the side of the road beyond the first casino. It was set out on a length of tracks only slightly longer than the Pullman itself, so God only knows how it wound up here. The cook, who also waited on customers seated on stools at the counter, introduced himself as Timothy. He was glad to make conversation while he fried up what the menu, set out in chalk on a blackboard, described as charcoal broiled hamburgers. (I couldn't spot any charcoal, just a gas-lit flame under a metal plaque, but as Ornella was paying for the solids, I didn't make a fuss.) "Ruggeris are the ones across the highway," Timothy explained, slipping a spatula under the burgers and flipping them over with a flick of his wrist. "Baldinis are on this side."

"Do they ever cross over and talk to each other?" I asked half in jest.

"Hell, no. I been here four years and I ain't even seen them meet in the middle. I'm answering your joke with a joke, right? Although my joke's no laughing matter—these guys pretty much keep to their own side of the tracks even though there ain't no tracks in Clinch."

"How did this Pullman wind up in the middle of nowhere if a railroad didn't run through here?" I asked.

"Search me," Timothy said. "It was parked here when I arrived. The guy who sells vegetables from the roadside stand a ways up the road was using it to store empty crates when I bought it. I did everything you see myself—the lampshades, the window curtains, the red leather banquettes over there, the brass rail under the windows. Everything's original except the red leather. I had to use vinyl because genuine leather was too pricey."

"You are a man for all seasons," Ornella remarked.

"Beg pardon?"

"It's an expression," Ornella said.

"It's a compliment," I assured him. "She thinks you're the cat's meow."

Ornella poked me with an elbow. "You may be older than I thought," she quipped.

When it was good and dark outside we settled up with

Timothy—I got the liquids, Friday the solids—then climbed back into the Toyota. "Where to now?" Ornella asked.

"Ever notice how parking areas outside of supermarkets or drive-ins or casinos look like used car lots? We're going vintage-car hunting."

When I could get across the road, which wasn't all that easy with all the traffic, I steered the Toyota into the Ruggeri lot and, moving at a crawl, started up one lane and down another and then up a third.

"You looking for any particular make of vintage car?" Ornella asked.

"Cadillac," I said.

I spotted the off-white Cadillac in the section marked RESERVED FOR CASINO PERSONNEL. I pointed it out to Ornella. "That's a 1938 LaSalle coupe," I said. "The teardrop fenders went out of style after the war. There may be only two hundred of these babies rolling today."

"How do you know so much about vintage cars?"

"I own one—my Studebaker is a 1950 Starlight. This Cadillac caught my eye. Wait here. Keep the motor running."

With Ornella watching from the Toyota, I made my way between parked cars to the Cadillac, took out my key to the Once in a Blue Moon and carefully scratched the left front teardrop fender from end to end. The sound was music to my ears.

When I got back to the Toyota, I found Ornella watching me through her night-vision goggles. "You were right about the goggles," she said. "Everything looks as if it's underwater. You looked as if you were swimming when you came back to the car." She gestured toward the Cadillac. "Why were you messing up a perfectly nice green Cadillac?"

I slid back behind the wheel of the Toyota. "It's biblical," I said. "An eye for an eye, a tooth for a tooth."

The penny dropped. "Oh, I get it. A fender for a fender! Now I know where the scratch on your Studebaker comes from. That's the famous Mario's Cadillac." Ornella studied me through her night-vision goggles. "Actually, you look good green." She took off the goggles and fitted them back into their case. "So you think vengeance is okay?"

I was following the arrows marked WAY OUT on the tarmac. "I'm not saying it's okay, I'm only saying that it's satisfying."

"As satisfying as crushing the metal cap of a beer bottle between your fingers?"

"As," I agreed.

We were waiting for traffic to let up so we could cross back to the Baldini side of the highway. The headlights of passing cars turned the front window of the Toyota opaque but filled the interior of the car with yellowish light. I became aware of how dirty the car was, crumbs, stains, smudges everywhere. I became aware of the fleeting smile performing live on Ornella's lips—it conveyed trepidation, or was it anticipation? Hard to tell as the two are kissing cousins. We often dread that we'll get what we think we want. Lemuel Gunn, the philosopher-detective, running off at the mouth again! I caught Ornella having a conversation with herself. She repeated the word "satisfying" a few times, sometimes with a question mark after it, sometimes with an exclamation point.

Punctuation, as they say in the gag trade, is everything.

I finally managed to cross back across the highway and pulled into a parking space near the Baldini casino. Water cascaded down man-made falls on either side of the gaudy main entrance. Two doormen wearing livery that went out of fashion in the Middle Ages tugged open the enormous imitation bronze doors with sculpted nymphs cavorting in their birthday suits on them. The effect was about as sensual as flushing out a septic tank with a self-priming pump.

I know what sucks good people into these giant hangars of iniquity, with their floor-to-ceiling windows draped in thick curtains so customers won't know it's morning and time to go home: It's unadulterated greed, it's the get-rich-quick, bet-now, pay-never mindset that has polluted the American spirit. Something tells me this is not what our ancestors were looking for when they crossed the Continental Divide. The presence of more losers than winners on the casino premises on any given night doesn't seem to discourage customers from thinking this is their night to break the bank. Which is to say the great majority of bettors checked their brains at the door. Prosecution exhibit number one: an intense young woman dressed in a particularly short mini-outfit methodically inspecting the slot machines trying to figure out which one was due to come up triple sevens. Two rows down, people flocked to congratulate a gray-haired woman when her one-armed bandit started spitting quarters into her paper cup. Overhead a siren yowled and the voice of an excited jerk of an MC boomed over the loud-speaker, "Ladies and gents, we have got us a *winner* in aisle four!"

I bought Ornella ten dollars' worth of quarters and parked her at one of the one-armed bandits. "If you win big, you do solids *and* liquids," I said.

"You going to be long?" Ornella asked worriedly.

It's been a while since anyone besides Kubra worried about me. "That depends," I said.

"Depends on what? Depends on whom?"

"On whether the local godfather, Giancarlo Baldini, will buy into my sales pitch."

"What are you selling, Lemuel?"

"Vengeance."

I looked around to get my bearings. You couldn't miss the bozos in shiny tuxedos posted around the floor like potted plants that only needed occasional watering. You had to be naive not to realize that the two young women in low-slung dresses giggling about how much they won were casino shills trying to lure bettors over to the roulette wheels. You had to be brain dead not to notice the long, narrow mirror high in the wall above the tables—it was the one-way mirror behind which the casino's professional gamblers watched for players who might be cheating the house. And you had to be blind not to spot the narrow door at the back of the hangar of iniquity and the lean, mean thug guarding it. A white wire snaked up from his starched collar to the tiny receiver in his ear, from time to time he spoke into a microphone on the inside of his left wrist. Nobody went through the door without him checking first with someone inside.

That was the portal to seventh heaven. Or maybe seventh hell.

I lingered at one of the blackjack tables long enough to watch a totally bald man double down on nines, which was probably his lucky number, and lose both hands to the dealer's back-to-back jacks. I moseyed over to the roulette tables and stood for a while behind a young man wearing designer blue jeans and farmers' suspenders jotting down the winning numbers in a minuscule notebook, as if the past of a roulette wheel could provide information about its future. Red or black. Odd or even. Go figure.

I drifted over to the narrow door.

"'Sup?" the lean, mean thug demanded.

I wasn't immediately able to translate his question into the king's English but I offered what I thought might pass for an explanation of my presence there. "I need to talk to Giancarlo Baldini," I said.

"He know you?"

"He would like to know me."

"You a wiseguy or something? Mr. Baldini don't appreciate wiseguys."

"I am answering your questions to the best of my ability."

"Name?"

"Gunn, with two *n*'s. I'm a private eye."

The lean, mean thug said something to his wrist. He must have gotten an answer because he glanced up at the long, narrow mirror and nodded. "They need to know about what you want to talk to Mr. Baldini," he said.

I looked up at the mirror and snapped off a casual Kabul two-finger salute, then turned back to the thug. "Tell them I want to talk to Mr. Baldini about the murder of his son Salvatore. I want to talk to him about the guy who set up Salvatore, Silvio Restivo."

The *they* watching from behind the one-way mirror must have had a microphone near the door because it clicked open before the thug could repeat a word I said. He seemed as surprised as I was to discover the door ajar. He looked up again at the mirror, listened to the tinny voice in his earpiece with his mouth drooping open, then reluctantly backed up to let me by. I walked into a white vestibule with small spotlights embedded in the ceiling and two more lean, mean thugs with BALDINI and CLINCH CORNERS emblazoned over the zippered pockets of their immaculate white jumpsuits. Both of them had skintight surgical gloves on their hands, which, I have to admit, made me uncomfortable—for a moment I was afraid they might be proctologists posted there to explore body cavities. Happily they concentrated on the usual places where firearms might be concealed when they frisked me: ankles, inner thighs, three-sixty degrees of waistband, small of back, armpits. I can say that the body search was very professional. I can see how when you do only one thing—when you specialize in patting people down, for instance—you wind up doing it well. One of them, a smirk of apology on his face, even threaded his fingers through my hair. Seeing I was weapon-free, he pushed a button in the wall and an elevator door opened. I stepped into it and turned back to confront the closing doors. The elevator rose one floor with excruciating slowness. The doors finally opened onto an enormous circular room with a high ceiling. What I took to be stereophonic Italian opera came at me from every direction. Off to my left, an accountant type wearing a green eyeshade was counting out stacks of money piled on a billiard table and securing each stack with a paper band. Off to my right, a very saddle-soaped saddle sat on a wooden trestle. Two teenagers dressed in identical blue school uniforms and ties were kneeling on cushions playing checkers on the floor. An ancient gentleman with a long beaked nose and a shirt that was several sizes too large for his neck—or had his neck shriveled since he bought the shirt?—sat in a wheelchair between them, tapping the squares on the board with the tip of his cane to suggest moves. Facing me, sitting in a plush leather swivel chair behind a shiny mahogany desk and in front of a picture window that followed the curve of the wall, was a young man with a face so pinched it looked as if it had been resized in a vise. Two computers were open on the desk in front of him. "You want to talk to Mr. Baldini," he said, "you need to talk to me first."

Getting past Baldini's gatekeepers was turning out to be almost as difficult as getting past Fontenrose & Fontenrose secretaries. I approached the desk. "I'm used to working through a chain of command," I said.

"You said your name is Gunn. You said you're spelling Gunn with two *n*'s."

"I have a New Mexico private investigator ID, if you want to see it."

He leaned forward to read something on the screen of one of his computers. "There are seventy-three Gunns listed. Three of them are associated with the words 'private investigator.' One of the private investigators name of Gunn lives in Hawaii and is twenty-two years old. That's not you. The second is an actor named Gunn who plays a private investigator in a television series. That's not you. Which narrows it down to the third private investigator named Gunn. First name, Lemuel. No middle initial. Forty-eight years of age. This particular Gunn runs a shoestring detective operation out of a mobile home in Hatch, New Mexico. Before that he was registered as a Department of State security officer stationed in Kabul, Afghanistan. Before that he was a detective sergeant assigned to the homicide division of the New Jersey State Police." Pinched Face looked up. "That's you, right? Department of State security officer is a common CIA legend. When did you stop being CIA?"

I figured why lie. "When I left Afghanistan."

"Why did you stop being CIA?"

"Management and I disagreed about something."

"What thing?"

"Murder."

"Who murdered whom?"

"A half-assed lieutenant murdered the Taliban who taught English to Osama bin Laden. His men murdered the Taliban's wife and two daughters."

"War is hell," Pinched Face said.

"Isn't it," I agreed. "Did you really find all that stuff about me on your computer?"

"I Googled you."

"What does that mean, you Googled me?"

"You want computer lessons, you go to a computer school. What do you want to tell Mr. Baldini about Salvatore and that scumbag Silvio Restivo?"

"What I have to say is for Mr. Baldini's ears."

"You're talking to Mr. Baldini's ears. I am his second son. My name is Ugo Baldini. The late Salvatore was my older brother."

"King me," one of the teenager checker players said excitedly.

"Hold on," the other checker player said. "You've got to jump me first."

"King him, damn it," the old man in the wheelchair told the first boy.

"But he—"

"Nuts to your buts," the old man said. He spoke in a wheezing whisper. "Do it now, Fabio."

Ugo looked at the checker players. "When I was your age I kept my mouth zipped."

"Sorry, Uncle Ugo."

"It won't happen again, Uncle Ugo."

"You'd think they was raised in a sewer," the old man wheezed.

Uncle Ugo acknowledged the apologies with raised eyebrows. He turned his attention back to me. "What do you know about Silvio Restivo that my father doesn't know?"

"I know where he's been for the eight months since Salvatore was shot to death."

"Where would that be, Mr. Gunn?"

"He was tucked away in an FBI witness protection program."

Ugo snickered politely. "You're not telling us anything we don't know."

"The Feds gave him a false identity."

The two boys kneeling on cushions stopped playing checkers and looked up. The ancient man had a toggle steering device on one arm of his wheelchair—there was a soft whirring noise as he backed and rotated and drove around the checker players to be nearer to Uncle Ugo's desk. He thumped the tip of his cane on the floorboard to get my attention. "You can identify this false identity?"

I turned my head and spoke directly to Giancarlo Baldini. "Yes, sir, I can. He was listed as Emilio Gava. He lived under that name in a condominium called East of Eden Gardens in Las Cruces, New Mexico."

The ancient man drove his chair so close he had to look up at me. "He still there?"

"No, sir. He got himself arrested on a drug charge, after which a woman put up a phony deed to guarantee bail and he was released. I work for the people who put up the actual bond and stand to lose $125,000 if Gava doesn't show for trial."

"Emilio Gava is not going to show up nowhere," the old man said. "Take my word for it, he was disappearing from the FBI's disappearment program." Mr. Baldini backed up his chair and spoke to Ugo. "Get the boys out of here. And turn that damn opera music off. I cannot hear myself think."

Ugo motioned with his chin. The accountant flicked a switch on the hi-fi behind him, collected the two boys and shooed them into the elevator. Giancarlo Baldini wheeled himself behind the desk. Ugo bounded to his feet and moved off to one side. I noticed the reflection of his ramrod-straight back in the curved window behind him. I'd seen soldiers stand to attention like that in Kabul when body bags were being loaded onto state-bound planes. It was obvious who was in command here.

"If I hear you right," Giancarlo Baldini said, "you know where Restivo *was* at. The question I have for you, do you know where he *is* at?"

"I'm thinking maybe we can figure this part out together," I said.

Mr. Baldini's eyes, what you could see of them with the soft lids of an old man half closed, clouded over with what I took to be hate. "When I was growing up in Palermo," he said, short of breath, wheezing to beat the band, "we used to say revenge was a dish that tastes best cold. I been waiting eight months to get my hands on Silvio Restivo. I do not plan to die before I do." He jabbed his cane in my direction. "Start at the start."

"When he was living in East of Eden, he used a neighbor's telephone to call a onetime girlfriend in Searchlight."

"We know all about this Annabel," Ugo said from the

corner of the desk. He looked at his father. "We tapped into her mobile, Dad—there were no calls from Restivo."

"He called her at the beauty parlor where she worked," I explained.

Mr. Baldini turned on his son. "Why didn't you think of that?"

Ugo just glared at me.

I said, "Annabel was the middleman between Restivo and someone named Mario in the Ruggeri stable."

"Stable is the right word," Mr. Baldini sneered. "They are all up to their backsides in horseshit."

"Mario is Mario Caruso," Ugo said. "He's their purse-string consigliere. He cooks their books."

"He may have been paying off Restivo for services rendered," I said. "The reason I think that is Annabel was passing on numbers. They could have been Swift numbers and bank account numbers."

"They was paying the scumbag off for fingering my boy Salvatore," Mr. Baldini said. He was practically choking on the words. Maybe I was imagining it but I thought I detected a tear in his voice.

"It figures," Ugo said. "Small amounts in different banks so as not to attract attention."

I couldn't resist asking, "How much is small?"

Mr. Baldini answered for his son. "Small is small. Small is ten, twenty grand." He tapped the tip of his cane on the desk in front of Ugo. "You need to have someone have a conversation with this Annabel person—"

"Talk to her from now to doomsday," I said, "you won't get more out of her than I got. She wrote down numbers and read them to Restivo over the phone and threw them out afterward."

Ugo was nobody's fool. "Maybe Mr. Gunn here has another lead," he said. "Maybe that's why he came looking for you, Dad."

Mr. Baldini's beak nose twitched as he eyed me. "You got another lead you want to share with us, Gunn?"

"As a matter of fact, there was something else Mario passed on to Annabel and Annabel passed on to Restivo," I said. "Does the word 'whistlestop' mean anything to you, Mr. Baldini?"

Mr. Baldini was ancient and serving out what was left of his life in a motorized wheelchair, but he had all his marbles. "Whistlestop," he repeated, "don't ring no bell—but it will. If it is a place, we will find it. If it is Silvio Restivo, we will wring his neck."

"Listen, if you wring his neck, you'll have your revenge that tastes best cold," I said. "The downside is that the truce between the Baldinis and the Ruggeris is hanging by a thread. If you kill Restivo, the Ruggeri family will consider the truce broken. You'll be starting a new cycle of tit-for-tat killings in Clinch Corners. Your family business interests—your casino—will suffer. Another round of clan warfare and the Nevada authorities, who don't bother you as long as you pay your taxes and keep a low profile, will come down on you like a ton of compacted automobiles. The families up in Reno won't be too happy either. The last thing they want is for some Palermo family to give the state a bad name."

"He's right," Ugo told his father. "That's not how they settle grudges in Reno. We need to keep the lid on. As long as we keep the lid on, nobody hassles our casino operation."

Mr. Baldini turned on his son. "I do not need lessons on how to do business from you, sonny boy." He worked the controls on the arm of his wheelchair and drove it closer to the curved windows, which looked out on the endless procession of red taillights heading back toward Los Angeles after a night of gambling. His wheezing voice drifted back over one of his withered shoulders. "So what are you proposing, that we leave Restivo live so as not to kill business?"

I said, "Mr. Baldini, when you decode 'whistlestop,' I'll take care of him for you."

His wheelchair whirred as the old man came around to face me.

I said, "I'll take him back to stand trial on the drug charge, Mr. Baldini. He'll pull ten, fifteen years for that. And there's an FBI officer who is persuaded Restivo set up your son for the sniper. He'll get a turn at him, too. One way or another he'll wind up behind bars for a very long time."

"He makes sense," Ugo said. "Once Restivo's safely in prison, we have ways—"

"I don't need to know what's going to happen to him in prison," I told Ugo. "In the CIA, we used to have a rule of thumb—don't share information with someone if it's above his pay grade."

The old man wheezed as he weighed the fate of Silvio Restivo. "What is your pay grade, Gunn?" he inquired when he got his wind. "What's in it for you?"

"I get ninety-five dollars a day plus expenses," I said. "I supply receipts for the expenses."

The younger Baldini scrutinized the expression on my face. "He is not making a joke," he told his father.

"I need Restivo to take a fall," Mr. Baldini said. "Then I can pass away in peace. In the good old days vigilantes who brought in killers got paid a bounty. You organize Restivo's fall, Gunn, there will be a packet in it for you."

"A not-so-small amount in an out-of-the-way bank," Ugo said.

Nobody shook hands when I left. Ugo stabbed at the button on the wall with his pinky. The elevator doors sprang open as if they'd been expecting the summons. "You and your lady friend come back this time tomorrow," Ugo said. "By then we'll know who or what or where this 'whistle-stop' is."

I did my best to look perplexed. "What lady friend?"

"The one you parked at the slot machine." Ugo smiled a compact smile that fitted nicely onto his pinched face. "I take it we are on the same page, Mr. Gunn?"

I shrugged one shoulder. "I think we are."

He looked at me peculiarly. "You're a piece of work, Lemuel no middle initial Gunn from Hatch, New Mexico,

Twenty-one

With the two other couples overnighting in Nipton—
dog-tired, dewy-eyed honeymooners from upstate New
York and older evangelicals (judging from the giant 3-D
crucifixes painted on the sliding doors of their minibus)
driving to L.A. to see the palm prints of film stars on the
sidewalk—we scrounged rations and beer in the general
store and fried up burgers on the stove in the hotel's common room. There was some strained table talk as the people
we were breaking bread with tried to figure out where the
others were coming from, I'm not talking geographically.
The evangelicals, who hailed from a small pushpin-in-the-
map township in Iowa, didn't turn around the pot for long.
"I couldn't help but notice you're not wearing a wedding
band," the woman remarked to Ornella. "You and your
friend here common-law husband, wife?"

"Not that it's any of your business," I said, "but we're
lover and lovee."

"Don't pay attention to him," Friday said without missing a beat. "He's cranky because we're winding down an
eight-year marriage." She smiled one of her cheerless signa-

waltzing in here with a cockamamie scheme to take out the rat who set up my brother Salvatore."

"You are, too, Ugo Baldini from Clinch Corners, Nevada, for taking me seriously."

ture smiles. "It may seem over-the-top sentimental," she went on, "but hey, as we're both big fans of Clara Bow, we decided to consummate the divorce in her bedroom."

Ornella said it all with such a straight face the others couldn't tell if she was pulling their leg or what. The honeymooners got it before the evangelicals. They grinned, then began laughing so hard the girl got hiccups. "That's rich," the young man allowed. "*Consummate* a divorce! I totally gotta try that out on my mother-in-law."

"Henry, don't—hic—go there," his young wife admonished.

After supper Friday and I crossed the railroad tracks and walked out into the dunes under an awning of desert stars that somehow managed to look as if they were shooting without even moving. Ornella quoted a line from an English poet whose name didn't mean anything to me at the time and is lost to me now—something about stars still dancing. Obviously the poet had been looking at the same stars as us but seeing them better. We settled onto the overhang of one groundswell of a dune and watched the last of a last-quarter moon skulk out of sight into the haze obscuring the horizon—it left a track of light in the sand glistening like the wake of a ship at sea, not that I've ever seen the wake of a ship at sea. My luck, I've always crossed oceans by plane. Just before eleven, one of those endless freight trains passed between us and Nipton. It was so long it needed two locomotives to inch it across the surface of the planet Earth. Once it had gone by we crossed back over the tracks and bedded down for the night in the Clara Bow room.

I thought again about the meeting with the Baldinis, godfather and son. I thought about the withered old man trapped in a motorized wheelchair. "What does 'Googled' mean?" I asked my girl Friday.

"Where did you pick up 'Googled'?"

"From Baldini's son Ugo. He had computers on his desk. One of them told him who I was."

She explained something about a search locomotive, whatever that was. I must have drifted off midexplanation because I still don't know what 'Googled' means. What I do remember is that I fell asleep—*we* fell asleep—without consummating our divorce. How relaxed can you get, sleeping in the Clara Bow bed with a female of the species, especially an extremely attractive specimen, without making whoopee?

I can't speak for Friday. For me it was an exhilarating experience.

At first light we rectified the lapse of the night before.

Fortified by steaming mugs of coffee and home-baked raisin muffins at the general store, we set out to explore the Mojave. I bought five plastic bottles of Poland Spring water (which I doubt came all the way from Poland but what the heck, they quenched thirst) and borrowed a desert kit from the hotel—a tire gauge and small compressor that worked off the Toyota's cigarette lighter, a folding army shovel, two metal tire tracks and a tarpaulin—and we hit the road. I'd had three weeks of survival training when I joined the CIA, it'd been in the Painted Desert, north of the Mojave, but if you've survived one desert you survived them all. The dunes, the flora and fauna, the dry wadis that curl out of wind-weathered canyons, the highways of tamped-down sand with the treads of tires printed on them, the drifts of heat rising off the ground—holy cow, for a boy raised on the Jersey Shore, I must have been a desert rat in another incarnation. How else do I explain that I felt at home where there were no homes?

With Friday riding shotgun, we drove southwest to an abandoned Union Pacific railroad crossing called Kelso Depot. It had a long wooden boom from the days when passing steam engines needed a refill of H_2O. We couldn't resist inspecting the Depot's abandoned hotel. Worn, torn shutters hung off rusted hinges, banisterless stairs wound up to the *bel étage* with gaping holes in its floorboards, a barrel of rainwater sat under a broken gutter on the half of the front porch that still existed. All of this only a few yards from the tracks along which long freight trains still passed.

Emerging from the hotel, Ornella had a faraway look in her eye. "What if . . ." she said.

"What if what?"

"What if we were to pool our money and buy this hotel. It'd probably go for a song. We could fix it up, turn it into a bed and breakfast, organize day trips into the Mojave on camels or jeep—"

We were standing on the good half of the front porch. I pushed a railing and it gave way, splintering off, falling onto the ground. "It'd go for half a song," I said. Friday's seaweed green eyes grew dark with disappointment. "Listen, I like pipe dreams as much as the next man," I said. "Let's keep dreaming them, the both of us."

"You never told me your pipe dreams," Ornella said.

"It'll come, little lady. Give it time."

I drove across the railroad tracks and pulled off the paved road onto a rise above Kelso Depot to let some air out of the tires, then went off-road onto desert trails, and then off-trail into the dunes. At one point a wind came up, nearly blinding us with sand. It felt as if we had driven into a wind tunnel, I needed both hands on the steering wheel to keep the Toyota on what I could see of the track. The wind died down as suddenly as it had come up. Except for an occasional exclamation—*oh, wow, will you look at that!*—Ornella was awed into silence most of the time, taking in the spectacular expanse with its ever-shifting horizon as if she was trying to memorize it. I pulled up on a flat deep in a canyon so we could give our backsides a rest and stretch our legs.

"You've been in the desert before," Ornella said. "I could tell from the way you drive."

"How do I drive?"

"You slalom over the dunes. You seem to feel where the steering wheel wants to go with your fingertips and don't fight it."

"I go with the flow," I admitted.

"What would you do if the Toyota broke down? Now. Here."

"I'd survive."

"You know how to survive in the desert?"

"I was taught. Look at the dry bed of the wadi over there. If you dig at the edges, you'd find wet sand. If you squeezed it in a handkerchief, you could moisten your lips."

"What about food?"

"Food's not a problem. You can survive two, three weeks without food. You couldn't survive two, three hours in the desert without water."

"We could drink the water in the Toyota's radiator," Ornella said brightly.

"That's a chemical refrigerant," I said. "It'd kill you for sure."

"Hey, people stranded in the desert can always drink urine."

I had to laugh. "Urine is better than nothing. But if you didn't have a container, you'd need to be two."

"Oh! Ooohhh. Aw. I didn't think of that aspect. It's pretty sexual."

"Best thing, if we were really lost in the desert, would be to make a still. Urine is ninety-five percent water. You dig a hole yea deep, you put your container—a glass, a pan, whatever—at the bottom and pee into it. Cover the hole with a tarp, a poncho, whatever you have handy. Weigh down the sides with sand or stones. Put one stone in the middle of the poncho so it sags down to the glass of urine but doesn't touch it. The sun will do the rest. After a while the water in the urine will condense on the underside of the tarp. You could lick it off with your tongue."

"Hey, if I'm ever lost in the desert, I want to be lost with you."

"That's the best offer I've had today," I said.

She looked at me queerly. "Does that mean you accept?"

I looked back at her queerly. "I accept," I said, "to get lost in the desert. With you. Now. Here."

And I did. Slaloming down and around and up giant dunes, I lost track of time and place and direction. I drove into a dry gulch that narrowed too much to pass—to Friday's delight I had to give up and back out. I pushed the Toyota up a stone slope and over the rim of one canyon, the sun slanting in over my right shoulder and then in my face and then over my left shoulder.

"You're not the same man here," Ornella announced as we crossed a washboard flat filled with wildflowers as far as the eye could see.

I understood what she meant. It was a different universe, which brought out a different side of anyone crossing through it. But I was curious to hear her take on this. "How, different?" I asked.

She didn't answer right away. Finally, she said, "You're not as angry. With the world. With me. You're not as disappointed. In the world. In me."

"What makes you think I'm disappointed in you?"

She smiled that smile. "I've got the antennas of a blind termite. I can *feel* your eyes on me when you suppose I'm not looking. I think you're judgmental. You judge yourself. You judge the people around you. You judge the girls you sleep with. You judged those evangelicals back at Nipton."

"You're coming down pretty hard on me, Friday."

"I'm not as hard on you as you are on yourself."

"That's a lot of insight considering you've only slept with me two nights."

"Best way to know someone," she said lightly. "That's what fucking's all about. You can figure out an awful lot about someone from the way he eats and dances and fucks."

"I'm not comfortable with that word," I said.

"When it describes what we do in the Clara Bow bed, I am," she said. "I'm not a virgin, Lemuel. I've had sexual experiences where the word 'fuck' would be too genteel a description to be appropriate."

"I'm sorry to hear that."

"I'm sorry if I'm shocking you."

"Since Afghanistan, I think of myself as unshockable."

In the late afternoon, when I finally was obliged to navigate, I raised my wrist with my father's Bulova and aimed the hour hand at the sun—halfway between that and the Roman twelve on the watch's face was due south. I turned my back on due south and, halfheartedly, pointed the Toyota in the direction of what some people think of as civilization.

Twenty-two

It was ladies' night at the Baldini casino—a rabble of them
had been bussed in from the Greater Los Angeles sprawl in
the top-heavy double-deckers lined up like dominoes near
the gas station. If one of them were to tip over, twelve or
fifteen would definitely go over after them. To the exasperation of the doormen in livery, two very inebriated young
pigwidgeons were washing their long hair in the man-made
waterfalls on either side of the imitation bronze front doors.
I was glad I'd decided to park Ornella in the Pullman diner
because there wasn't a free slot machine in sight inside. The
sound of one-armed bandits paying off enough to keep the
saps coming back for more reverberated from the loudspeak-
ers overhead. I plunged through the perfume scents that contaminated the casino's recycled air to the narrow door at the
back. The same lean, mean thug was on duty. He looked
daggers at me as the door clicked open before I could salute
the long rectangular mirror over the tables. "You don't cheer
up," I told him as I edged past his tuxedo bib, "I'll think
I'm not welcome here."

There were two different proctologists in the elevator vestibule on this visit. They proceeded to frisk me as if I was registered with the FBI as a Ruggeri soldier. When the elevator doors parted at the first floor, Ugo was waiting, a quizzical expression on his pinched face. He wasn't standing to attention. There was no opera playing on the hi-fi. An empty wheelchair was parked next to the trestle. Giancarlo Baldini was astride the horse's saddle set up on it. He wore a short cream-colored cape over a dark suit several sizes too big for him—or was he several sizes too small for it? His cuffed and creased trousers were tucked into felt ankle-length zipper slippers. "My doctor ordered me to exercise," he called across the room, "so I climb into the saddle and remember what it was like to ride a horse." He was wheezing more than I remembered, which made me think he'd overdone the exercise bit. Ugo waved me to a straight-backed wooden chair that had been dragged over to the elevator side of the mahogany desk. He walked around it to settle into the swivel chair and did a slow three-sixty until he was facing me again. The accountant type from the night before, minus the green eyeshade, lifted the old man off the saddle, lowered him into the wheelchair and tucked a tartan quilt up to his hips. The motor whirred. Mr. Baldini senior almost collided with my legs in his eagerness to pick up the conversation where it had left off.

"Whistlestop," he rasped.

"Whistlestop," I repeated.

"Whistlestop is not a person. It is a goddamn place. It's

the name of the fancy bar at a new Ruggeri spin-off the other side of the Arizona border in Bullhead City. 'Whistle-stop' as in 'stop and wet your whistle.'"

"My dad doesn't miss a trick," Ugo said from behind the desk. "It's a closed-door, invitation-only, high-stakes Texas hold 'em poker operation run out of the top floor of what used to be a house of ill repute—"

"What is this 'house of ill repute' crap," Mr. Baldini snapped. "A whorehouse is what it used to be until the Rug-geris fancied it up with a permanent poker game."

"Silvio Restivo is in there somewhere," Ugo said. "He's a dealer, he's a house gambler, he's a floor boss. He must have been going stir-crazy in the FBI witness thing. So he broke out of their protection prison. Maybe he's dealing, maybe they put him in charge of the hold 'em poker tables to pay him back for setting up Salvatore. Whichever." He leaned closer to the screen of one of his computers. "I Googled this new Ruggeri joint. The business runs out of a four-story building right across the Colorado River from Laughlin. Says here it was put up in the 1950s when the Bullhead Dam was being constructed and the town—all six blocks of it that ran north-south along U.S. 95—was crawling with workers looking to spend their paychecks." Ugo manipulated a small rodent-sized contraption on a pad next to the com-puter. "Okay, here we go. First two floors are the Whistle-stop bar and a river-view restaurant. Third floor is roulette, blackjack for the hoi polloi. Fourth floor is where the play is. Only big rollers with invitations get past the small army of Ruggeri soldiers guarding the door."

"Baldinis do not need an invitation to get past any door," the old man wheezed.

"From the sound of it," I said, "you'd have a truckload of corpses to dispose of if you tried to force your way in."

The old man squinted at me. "We have a certain experience in disposing of corpses," he said.

"Last time we talked," I reminded him, "you were on board for me to bring in Restivo."

He shifted into reverse. The gears made a grinding noise as he backed away from me. "Damn thing is only good for forward motion," he said. He said it in a way that made me think he had a certain amount of patriarchal savvy squirreled away in that Palermo-thick brain of his. He confirmed this intuition with the instructions he gave his son. "Fit Gunn out with five thousand in cash. Use newly minted large-denomination bills. He needs to be able to flash some significant hard currency to have a hope in hell of getting up to the Texas hold 'em floor." The old man observed me with watery eyes. "Consider it a down payment on the vigilante bounty you get for bringing in the rat Restivo. I need you to refund the money if you do not bring home the bacon. Understood?"

"Understood, sir."

Ugo looked at me across the desk. "You ever been to Bullhead City?"

I pursed my lips no.

"Don't blink," he warned, "or you'll miss it."

Twenty-three

Ugo was wrong. You couldn't have missed Bullhead City if
you catnapped at the steering wheel. There were the never-
ending acres of mobile home parks in the onetime alfalfa
fields around the kernel of the city that took its name from
the original dam on the Colorado River, which took its name
(according to a historical marker) from the famous Bull's
Head Rock upstream. Turned out that what must have been
thousands of mobile homes served as second homes for
folks fleeing colder climes in winter. There were two old billboards on 163 and dozens of posters peeling off speed-limit
and stop and school-crossing signs, all of them trumpeting
McCain for senator. We crossed the Colorado River at Laughlin and turned around some before we spotted the four-
story building just beyond the city-limit sign with a torn
McCain poster on it. The former house of ill repute stuck
out like a sore thumb on a spit of land that jutted into the
Colorado. Which left only one paved road—pretty much a
causeway—to reach the Ruggeris' spin-off operation.

I had a game plan. Friday was a key player.

Since she'd been the one to meet with Silvio Restivo,

a.k.a. Emilio Gava, when she posted $125,000 worth of bail for him, which turned out to be his get-out-of-jail-free card, I decided she needed to disguise herself so the perpetrator, if he was really inside this building, wouldn't recognize her when she recognized him.

I made an illegal U-turn and we headed back to town, skirting a Wal-Mart and a K-mart, skirting a Home Depot. We got backed up in traffic passing a convention hall with a banner strung across the gate announcing the Bullhead Annual Chili Cook-off. It took us a while to reach the Sears lot. I waited in the Toyota while Friday went shopping. I was lost in pipe dreams that could have doubled as PG fantasies when someone tapped at the passenger window. It was a young woman, though not all that young. She had on more makeup than the receptionist at Fontenrose & Fontenrose. She wore a sleeveless art-deco print of a dress that was unbuttoned down to her solar plexus, along with very small oval sunglasses that obscured the whites of her eyes but not the charcoal black on the lids above them. Thinking she wanted a lift or, worse still, to turn a quick trick, I wagged a finger at her. Her painted lips thinned into a smile I thought I'd seen before. But where?

Curiously, she had the same silver astronaut knapsack as Ornella Neppi slung over one lean shoulder.

"Hey, it's me. Open up, huh?"

I even recognized the voice, the intonation that often sent sentences spiraling off on a high note.

Of course it was Friday in the flesh (and there was more than a bit of it in evidence on her chest). It's nothing short of startling how a woman can renovate herself in forty-five minutes flat. The young woman tapping at the window of my rented Toyota had nothing in common with the Friday who had set out with me that morning dressed in loose-fitting overalls and basketball sneakers. What a difference a credit card at a Sears can make.

"How the heck did you pull that off?" I demanded as she slid in next to me (and I spotted the slit up the side of the skirt). She'd even doused herself with a not-so-cheap perfume that had nothing in common with the odors that contaminated the recycled air in the Baldini casino.

"Tricks of the trade," she said. She took off her sunglasses to edit some of the charcoal that had trickled into one of her lashes. I noticed the merriment dancing in her eyes. For an instant I could see what she must have looked like as a little kid on summer vacation in Corsica. "I told you I did miming gigs at birthday parties," she said. "Besides a toothbrush and toothpaste, that's what I lug around in my knapsack—disguises, a makeup kit, wigs, buck teeth, funny eyeglasses, a kazoo on which I play an almost unrecognizable version of 'Happy Birthday to You.' I even have a false nose for my act. Wait a sec, I'll put it on."

I put my hand on her wrist. "The false nose would probably be a nose too far," I said. "For Pete's sake, you could have waltzed into the Nipton general store at breakfast and I wouldn't have recognized the woman I'd spent the night with."

"Hey, that's the point of this exercise, isn't it?"

"Okay. What say we put this road show on the road."

Her mood changed as suddenly as a cloud dark with rain obscures the sun. "What say," she agreed, any trace of merriment veiled in bleakness.

We hit the causeway, which had speed bumps on it, and pulled up on the circular driveway in front of the Ruggeri spin-off in Bullhead City. Talk about understatement—a discreet bronze placard next to the front door read MEMBERS ONLY. Six or eight three-piece suits stood around, and a small sign on a board said VALET PARKING. One of the three-piece suits came around to the driver's side of the Toyota. "Good evening, Mr. Gunn," he said, bending to talk to me at eye level. "Welcome to Bullhead City's premier den of iniquity." He said it with a chillingly straight face.

"How do you know my name?"

"Someone called ahead to reserve a table for two in your name at the River View. Whoever called said you would be driving a dirty Toyota. If you'll leave the keys, we'll park the car. Sir, do you want us to wash it for you?"

"No, thanks. I drive better in dirty cars."

One of the valets opened the door for Friday, his eyes glued to the flash of thigh as she got out. She hooked one arm through mine and we made our way up the steps. "Open sesame," Ornella said, waving her free hand and lo and behold the front doors opened magically before us.

"What other magic tricks can you do?" I asked.

"I can make things disappear," she said. I looked quickly at her. She was dead serious.

We started at the spit-shined Whistlestop bar to wet our whistles where, abracadabra, Friday made two bone-dry martinis disappear down the hatch while I was still nursing an Alabama Slammer. Relishing the crisp comfort of cold cash, I paid for the drinks and the refills with a factory-fresh hundred-dollar bill.

"Ink dry on this?" the bartender asked, holding the image of Ben Franklin up to the light.

"It must be—made that myself last night and hung it out to dry in the warm breeze coming off the desert." Friday and I slid off our stools. "Keep the change," I said.

I could have sworn I saw the bartender talking into a house phone as we made our way up to the second-floor River View Restaurant. A table was set for two in a corner with a view of Laughlin across the Colorado and the gaudy River Palace, along with a handful of other medium-rise casino-hotel sore thumbs. A waitress wearing what might have passed for a cowgirl outfit when Douglas Fairbanks Jr. was living in my all-aluminum mobile home brought us two enormous menus. She stood balanced on one leg, holding on to one of her pigtails as if it were an overhead subway strap while we studied *le carte du jour*. We settled on shrimp cocktails, middling-hot chili con carne Mexican style washed down with two cold Negra Modelos, and finished up lingering over a steaming pot of geography-defying Nicaraguan Arabica.

For the record, I ought to say I was becoming accustomed to the presence of the other Ornella Neppi, the one in the Sears duds and short dark hair neatly tucked behind her ears. While she gazed through the window at Laughlin across the river I gazed at her art-deco print of a dress unbuttoned down to her solar plexus. She turned unexpectedly to find me groping her chest with my eyes. "You really want to see cleavage, I need to bend forward like this," she said. She leaned across the table until one of her breasts nearly fell out of her dress. "Girl stuff," she said very seriously. "We practice this sort of thing in front of a mirror till we get it down pat."

I looked around to see if anyone was looking. "You're embarrassing me," I said.

"Just clowning around—testing to see if you're embarrassable," she said, shrugging the breast back into the dress as she straightened in her chair. "This meal is going to set you back a pretty penny."

"How can you tell?"

"Easy. My menu didn't have prices on it. Hey, I hope you're not planning to put it on your expense account."

"Not going to set me or you back a pretty penny," I said. "You're forgetting the tab is being picked up by a couple of friends of mine over in Clinch Corners." I raised a finger for the check, which arrived in no time on a silver tray. The cowgirl who brought it was holding a contraption that swallowed credit cards and regurgitated receipts.

"Does this establishment accept cash?" I asked with snake-oil innocence.

"Last time I checked, we sure as heck did," the waitress said pleasantly.

I glanced at the check and folded three spanking new hundred-dollar bills onto her silver tray. "You'll be doing me a favor if you keep the change, dear," I said.

"Sure am glad to oblige a satisfied customer," she said.

"How can you tell I'm satisfied?"

Smiling a knowing smile, she looked from me to Friday and back to me. "Probably had something to do with the grin on your face during dinner."

"Aren't you overdoing the big-spender-from-the-East bit?" Friday remarked when the cowgirl was out of earshot.

I noticed our cowgirl whispering to the head waiter at the door of the restaurant. I waved my entire arm to attract his attention. I caught his eye and pointed so he'd know I meant him and not the waitress. He came waltzing over pronto. He waltzed adroitly, which I attributed to the Nike sneakers I spotted under his ankle-length white butcher's apron.

"Where can a gent find a little action in Bullhead City?" I asked.

"We have action that fits all sizes," he said. "Why don't you start at one of the blackjack tables upstairs. See where it goes."

"What do you say, darlin'? We could kill an hour at blackjack, then look around for something more stimulating."

"Blackjack for an hour is fine by me," Friday said.

Fact of the matter is I happen to be one hell of a blackjack player. I have a pretty fair idea of the odds going for the house and against the chumps putting down money, so it came as no surprise to me when, having bought a thousand dollars worth of chips from the cashier on the third floor of this members-only den of iniquity, having noisily flashed my thick wad of new hundred-dollar bills in the process, I found the stack in front of me growing taller.

"Surprise, surprise, you seem to know what you're doing," Friday said.

She was standing next to my left shoulder, the fingers of her right hand resting lightly on my right shoulder, her right breast brushing lightly against my left arm. The two parties to my left obviously caught the body language because both men sat there (losing steadily) with smug smiles plastered on their lips. I doubled down on aces, a red hundred-dollar chip on each of them, and pulled one blackjack and one nineteen, which beat the dealer's seventeen. Friday reached over to add the three hundred dollars' worth of chips to my stake, giving me a whiff of her perfume as she straightened my leaning stacks of Pisa with her delectably long fingers.

You can read a lot into the expression in someone's eyes. I could see from hers that she wasn't used to being on the winning team.

I glanced at my father's Bulova. Ha! He would have had to work a month of Sundays to accumulate what I'd won at blackjack in less than an hour. With studied casualness, one of the tuxedo suits patrolling the sanctum stopped to watch me play. He edged closer to whisper in my ear. "Not sure I should be telling you this, given this is your lucky day" is what he said. "If blackjack is too tame for you, there's a serious game of Texas hold 'em going on on the top floor."

"Don't say," I said. I turned to Friday. "You ever play Texas hold 'em?"

She shook her head no.

"Want to learn?"

She shrugged her shoulders why not.

I turned back to the tuxedo. "How does one get upstairs?"

"Staircase through the door behind that curtain," he said, pointing with his chin.

I collected my chips and dropped them into my jacket pocket. "What say we mosey on upstairs and take a look-see at this Texas hold 'em," I told Friday.

"What do we have to lose?" she said. She was looking around the room, studying the players, studying the tuxedos, studying the dealers as if she had a lot to lose.

The top floor of the four-story house of ill repute was two-thirds wraparound terrace and one-third private club consisting of sawdust on the floor and a clipper ship's worth of mahogany, a bar replete with spittoons and four green-felt poker tables set at right angles to each other and lit by shafts of light coming from the ceiling. Only two of the tables had activity around them. Gunn, the seeing-eye detective, counted two dealers and fifteen or so marks, the players totally riveted by the closed cards they'd been dealt, the kibitzers flirting with their lady friends or the lady friends of other kibitzers. From the masks of concentration on the faces of the players and dealers you would have thought I'd meandered into a crash course on string theory, I'm not talking bathing costumes. I began my sojourn on the fourth floor at the house bank, cashing in my fifty-dollar chips for two-hundred-dollar chips, adding eight five-hundred-dollar chips to my stake. I turned back to the tables and found an empty seat at one of them. Ornella stayed behind at the bar. The dealer acknowledged my presence with a curt nod. Including me, there were eight players at the table. I anteed up a hundred dollars to get into the game. He dealt me two hole cards. I peeked at the corners the way I'd seen serious gamblers do in movies, hiding them with my free hand, to discover a seven of spades and a four of hearts, nothing to make your heart beat faster. The dealer set out the flop, three cards faceup, a jack and an ace and a five of hearts, giving me hope for a straight or a flush, so I stayed in for another round before I folded, which set me back four hundred bucks. By the time the dealer dealt the river, the fifth and last open card, there were two players left and something like fifteen thousand dollars in the pot. A hostess appeared at my elbow to offer me a drink on the house. I said thanks but no thanks. I needed to keep my head clear and my hand steady. There was some heavy bidding when the flop hit the table the next hand. The gent I took for the house player upped the ante, bluffing the weak-kneed out, and eventually walked off with the pot—probably ten grand by then—with two pairs. "You in?" the dealer asked as my attention wandered. I tossed in a red chip. Cards came my way but I only had eyes for Friday, who was standing near the bar. She appeared to have frozen in her tracks. I folded as soon as I could and went over to her. She was staring across the room, her face as white, despite the blush-on blushed on with abandon in the Sears dressing room, as the white cliffs of Dover, not that I've ever seen the white cliffs of Dover. "'Sup?" I asked, having finally deciphered the coded question posed by the mean, lean thug guarding the Baldini elevator.

"It's him," she said, her normally musical voice stuck on a single note in the octave, her lips barely moving as she spoke.

"Gava?"

"Emilio in the flesh." She turned away and sucked oxygen through her nostrils as if it was in short supply.

"You're sure?"

She didn't turn back to double-check. "The house dude who climbed onto the high stool in front of the window, the one watching the tables—it's him. It's Emilio." She caught another quick look over her shoulder. "Jesus, he's changed. Though not changed so much that I wouldn't recognize him. He's the same but he's trying to look different. His hair is different. It was long and shiny black when he appeared before the judge, now it's short and dirty blond. He's wearing horn-rimmed eyeglasses. I never saw him wearing eyeglasses. He's grown a mustache—"

"Or glued one on."

She was getting a grip on her emotions. "What do we do now?" she whispered.

"You order another of your very dry martinis and nurse it. I play poker for a half hour. Win or lose, we skedaddle."

I returned to my seat at the table. From time to time I caught a glimpse of Gava, his head angled to one side as if he were hard of hearing in one ear, studying the players and the play from his high chair. He was obviously a pro, not to mention some kind of bigwig on the fourth floor because tuxedos kept coming over to check with him. Sometimes he nodded yes. Sometimes he nodded no. When he nodded yes the door at the back near the staircase would open and a new mark with or without a date was allowed into the room.

Luck was running with me at my hold 'em table for a while. I pulled a pair of nines in the hole and the river gave me a third one to take one hand, and hidden aces over the flop's double fours to squeak past two hole kings on another. Then the table turned against me. I dropped all of my winnings and most of my nest egg in five hands that I thought I could win. The guy I fixed to be the house player won them all. I watched the dealer's fingers closely but didn't see anything that looked out of the ordinary, though I reckoned a really good dealer could collect the cards and shuffle them till the cows came home and give them to me to cut, then deal them so that the house player wound up with a pair of aces and one more on the river. Go figure.

I noticed Friday had settled onto a bar stool. I smiled at her but she didn't smile back. Seeing the bail jumper in the flesh had discombobulated her. I pushed back my chair and climbed to my feet. "Too rich for me," I said. Two of the players laughed out loud in scorn, which made me want to take them down a peg or two, but I got a handle on my anger and went over to Ornella.

"What say we check out of this joint," I said. She seemed incapable of speech. I took her by the elbow and led her to the bank where I traded in the few chips left to me for cash.

One of the tuxedos held the door open for us. "Come back next time you're feeling lucky, Mr. Gunn."

Made me uncomfortable, everyone knowing my name. "Sure, why not? Your liquor's as good as anybody's and cheaper if you don't count what I lost at cards."

I didn't waste a smile on the tuxedo. He registered my failure to smile with a mean snicker. So it goes. You can't satisfy everyone.

Twenty-four

The art and craft of following someone from in front, by Lemuel Gunn, with two *n*'s. I didn't invent the technique but I don't deny I perfected it, offering (to my colleagues on the homicide gig in the New Jersey State Police) the rule of thumb that your chances of success increased if you worked the night shift, which was another way of saying that taillights tend to look alike in the dark; headlights on the other hand can be as distinctive as your lady's eyes. I'd parked the rented Toyota on a narrow residential street up from the causeway, which, you'll remember, was the only way into or out of the waterfront den of iniquity. Friday was supposed to be catching forty winks on the backseat. I caught a glimpse of her wide-open eyes every time the headlights of a passing car swept across my windshield spattered with the corpses of insects.

"Sleep comes easier if you shut your eyes," I remarked somewhere around two in the morning.

After a moment I heard her voice husky with fatigue drift over my shoulder. "My Corsican grandfather used to nap after lunch with his eyes wide open," she said. "You need to try it sometime."

I had parked near enough to the corner to keep an eye on the joint's front door. I could see the valet-parking dudes in three-piece suits ferrying cars around to the circular drive-way, I could see the marks and their lady friends climbing in and heading across the causeway, turning left as they came off it toward town. I was beginning to think that Gava a.k.a. Restivo the Wrestler might be spending the night with an elbow on the Whistlestop bar when I caught sight of a lean man with a mop of blond hair emerging from the building. He must have phoned ahead because the car, a black sport number of foreign manufacture judging by the low phallus-shaped silhouette, materialized as he reached the circular driveway. Gava chatted up the valet who had brought it around, laughing and punching him playfully in the chest before he climbed, feet first, into the racing car. From a distance it appeared as if he was fitting himself into riding boots. I could hear him gunning the motor from my perch two hundred yards away. His parking lights flicked onto bright and the machine growled its way across the causeway. I started the Toyota's motor but I didn't light off my headlights until I turned the corner onto the main drag, a football field ahead of Gava. I watched him gaining on me in my rearview mirror until Ornella, realizing some-thing was up, sat up.

"I need you to scrunch to one side or the other," I said. "Hard to follow someone from in front when you can't see out the back."

"Oh, sorry." She moved over. The racing car was closing the gap so I sped up just enough to stay discreetly ahead of him. Two cars fell into line behind him. After six or seven blocks, the phallus signaled a right turn. Speeding up, I continued on for another block, turned right at the corner and right two blocks down and right again onto a long stretch of classy postwar residential apartment buildings set back from the street. I was expecting to see a pair of headlights coming toward me. Nothing. I pulled up at the curb, cut the motor and the lights and leaned into the steering wheel, thinking.

"So you're supposed to be street-smart and lucky," Friday said encouragingly.

"Right now I'm running on lucky," I said. I had an idea. "Give me your mobile telephone and wait here."

I got out and started down the sidewalk, eyeing the parking spaces between hedges in front of each of the apartment buildings. At midblock I spotted the silhouette of the phallus tucked in for the night in a space with rose vines woven into an overhead trellis. Making my way to the building's lobby, I sidled past the phallus. It was a coal black Ferrari with red leather bucket seats, the hood over the motor was still pleasantly warm to the touch. In the dark I opened Friday's mobile telephone and removed the chip, then smiling to beat the band, walking very carefully as if I were a wee bit tipsy, went up the steps and pushed through the door into the lobby. There was an elderly black man with a light gray crew cut and a trimmed white beard behind the night desk, and a thick glass door between me and a bank of elevators through which nobody went unless the night man buzzed you through. "My pal dropped this climbing into his Ferrari at the fancy riverside casino joint," I said, holding out the mobile telephone. "Tried to catch up with him but couldn't gain on that racing car of his. Will you give this to him in the morning?"

"You mean Mr. Picone."

"Is there anyone else in Bullhead City drives a Ferrari?" I inpuired with what Kubra would have described as a knowing chortle.

The night man took the telephone from me and slipped it into a brown envelope and wrote on it *Mr. Picone 4C.* "I'll be off duty but the day man will give it to him. Who shall I say—"

I chortled again. "He'll know who left it here," I said. " 'Night."

" 'Night to you, sir."

"Emilio Gava's living in apartment 4C under the name of Picone," I told Ornella back in the car. She had slipped into the front passenger seat where I could see the white of her thigh through the slit in her dress.

"My friend was right about you," she said. "You're plenty street-smart and don't discourage easily. What you do, you do well."

"You're talking about finding a needle in a haystack," I said.

She smiled one of those mystifying smiles that I was still busy deciphering. "I'm talking about the way you make love," she said.

"Another compliment like that and I'll light up the car with one of my aw-shucks blushes."

I started the Toyota and headed back across the river to look for the all-night motel I'd spotted on the highway into Laughlin. After a while Friday murmured, "So where are we going?"

I was about to tell her when I noticed she'd fallen fast asleep. This time with her eyelids closed.

Twenty-five

I threw some cold water on my face and dialed Detective Awlson's home number at seven ten the next morning. "Expect I woke you," I said.

"Hell, no. I've been up for minutes," he shot back in what sounded like an imitation of Groucho Marx describing how he swept women off his own feet.

I told him I'd tracked Gava down to Bullhead City. I gave him the street address, the apartment number, the name he was registered under. "Can you come up with a phone number for this Picone in 4C?"

"When do you need it by?"

"Ten minutes ago."

"I'm on it," he said.

When I phoned back, Awlson had the number for me. "What you figurin' on doin'?" he asked.

"I'm going to go and wish him top of the morning," I said. "Stay tuned."

Friday was curled up in a fetal position on her side of the double bed, breathing heavily, snoring lightly. I propped up two pillows against the bed board and sat with my back to them, the motel telephone on my lap. I took a deep breath and exhaled and dialed nine for an outside line, then Picone's number in Bullhead City. The phone must have rung twenty, twenty-five times before someone got around to answering it.

"Christ sake, you know what time it is? Who the fuck is this?"

"It's someone who is going to save you a lot of grief," I said. "But it'll cost you an arm and a leg."

I thought I could make out Emilio Gava lighting a cigarette on the other end of the phone line. I caught the dry hacking cough of a smoker savoring that first morning drag. "Bullhead City passed a no-smoking ordinance a few days back, Emilio. If you're not careful you could be arrested for smoking in a no-smoking zone. R. Russell Fontenrose would have a hard time springing you from that rap."

"Who the fuck are you?"

"Let's skip the name-rank-serial-number bit and get down to job description. I'm a headhunter, Emilio. I've been tracking you across the country from the East of Eden poker condominium to that Blue Grass drug deal that got interrupted by three policemen to the courthouse where you walked on bail. Lot of folks would pay me handsomely to tell them where you are and who you are, Mr. Picone. Old man Baldini, for starters. The Las Cruces cop who arrested you at the Blue Grass. The girl who put up the $125K bail bond. The judge who let you out on bail thinking you would show up for trial. The FBI agent who runs the witness protection program you ran out on—he's convinced you can help him with his inquiries into the murder of one Salvatore Baldini."

Emilio must have been sucking on his cigarette because he didn't answer right away. "You still there?" I asked. "If you're thinking of running again, you won't get far in that Ferrari of yours. There probably isn't another car like that in the Far West."

"Talk turkey, huh? What you expect to get from me, Mr. Headhunter?"

"Money."

"How much?"

"Twenty-five grand. In crisp fifties and hundreds."

"I don't got that kind of dough at my fingertips."

"You have ten times that in the bank accounts the Ruggeris set up for you, slugger."

"Saying I go ahead with this, which I am not, how do I know you won't come back for sloppy seconds?"

"You don't. On the other hand you need to look at it from my point of view. This is a one-shot deal for me. Anything else wouldn't make sense. I don't want this to be the beginning of an ugly friendship, Emilio."

"Say I got the money, which I am not saying, you planning on coming around to collect it?"

"Don't play me for a chump, Restivo the Wrestler. You're coming to me."

"Where? When?"

Friday sat up in bed and tuned in to the conversation. She was wearing one of my T-shirts that was falling off one shoulder. "You talking to *him*?" she whispered. I nodded. To Emilio I said, "Midnight tonight."

"That don't leave me an awful lot of time," he whined.

"It leaves you a day's worth of banking hours," I said. I gave him directions from Bullhead City to Kelso Depot. I told him I'd be out in the desert watching the Ferrari come down the road through the AN/PVS-10 telescopic night sight of an M-24 army sniper rifle. I couldn't resist adding that I had reason to believe he knew how lethal a 175-grain hollow-point boat-tail round could be at half a mile. Ornella whispered in my free ear, "You've been reading too many detective novels." In my ear glued to the telephone, I heard Silvio say almost the same thing. "You sound like you seen too fucking many Humphrey Bogart pictures."

"With or without Bogart, I don't much like motion pictures."

"How can anyone not like flicks?"

"They distract us from real life, they don't console us about real life." I could tell we weren't on the same wavelength. "Listen up, Emilio, did you ever see a woman lift a suitcase in a motion picture that looked as if it had anything in it except air? Most of what's in pictures these days is as phony as these suitcases filled with air."

"What the fuck we talking about movies?" Emilio demanded. He answered his own question. "This conversation is nuts. You are nuts."

He was right, of course. It dawned on me that the last

thing I needed to do was tangle with this hoodlum nick-named the Wrestler. On the other hand, it was the first thing I needed to do if I wanted to get Ornella Neppi off the $125,000 hook she was hanging from. So I told Emilio about the abandoned hotel next to the railroad tracks at Kelso Depot. I told him to park his Ferrari a football field up the highway. I told him to leave the headlights and the interior lights on. I told him to walk to the hotel and leave the money under the staircase in what used to be the lobby. "Come alone," I said. "I see someone else within ten miles, the deal's off and your cover is blown, friend. At which point an old man in a wheelchair and his house proctologists will be breathing down your neck."

"What about after?" he asked.

"What *about* after?"

"After I leave off the dough, if I decide to leave off the dough, then what?"

"After, you turn around and walk back to your car and take your cue from the spider and disappear back into your hole in the wall."

I kept the phone to my ear but cut the connection with my thumb.

Ornella was impressed, which, looking back, I can see is what drove the dialogue between me and the bail jumper. "Wow!" she said softly.

I realized I'd been as tense as the night I'd staked out a Taliban safe house in Peshawar from a slit in the wall of the house across the alleyway. I had muscle cramps in the limbs that had muscles. I dropped the phone back on its hook and shook both my hands at the wrists the way I'd seen rock climbers do halfway up a cliff to get the blood flowing again.

"So you actually think he'll show up?" Ornella asked.

"I think he'll show up. I don't think he'll be carrying money."

"Is he dangerous?"

"Is a snake dangerous?"

"You're answering a question with a question, damn it."

"Right now that's the best I can do," I said.

Twenty-six

I'll do the Kelso Depot brawl now. It won't be pretty. Parental guidance recommended, whatever.

I'd driven the Toyota over the Kelso tracks and off-road into a wadi a good two miles from the abandoned hotel, then hiked back, with Friday slugging along behind me, to a dune that had a good view of the Depot and the single paved road across the Mojave Desert leading to it. We'd brought along packaged white bread and a tube of mayonnaise and two cans of sardines and several bottles of Poland Spring water for a spur-of-the-moment picnic, but neither of us had an appetite for anything given the violence to come. By the time the sun had sizzled into the Mojave, kicking up a momentary firestorm on the horizon, and darkness began blotting up what was left of daylight, I was stretched out on the tarpaulin watching through the army PVS-7 night-vision goggles Ornella had picked up at Millman & Son Hard and Soft Ware. The bluish green hues rising off the desert in drifts stirred unpleasant recollections of the Hindu Kush—it was almost as if I was again trapped underwater and struggling to rise to the surface before my breath ran out. Friday heard me sucking air through my lips.

"You all right, Lemuel?" she asked. She was stretched out faceup on the tarp alongside me, watching the planets and then the stars sending their Morse-coded messages from the dark dome over her head. The black wig was gone, stuffed back into her silver astronaut knapsack, the thick makeup had been scrubbed off with Poland Spring water, the high heels had given way to basketball sneakers, the Sears sleeveless art-deco dress had been pulled up above her knees and the fabric tucked between and under her thighs. Through my goggles, the V-shaped sliver of skin on her chest looked to be the same color as the welts from that automobile accident I'd seen on her ribs, a sickly bluish green. I reached across and slipped a palm under the fabric onto her breast. She pressed her hand over the fabric, over my hand, locking in the gesture, sealing a contract we had yet to make.

After a time she asked if I had ever used night-vision goggles in Afghanistan.

"Once."

"What did you see?"

"You don't want to know. I don't want to remember."

She didn't push the matter beyond where I wanted to go. I watched the luminous hands on my dad's Bulova, they moved so slowly I thought the watch might have stopped and tried winding the stem only to find it was wound. I watched the Big Dipper pivot around Polaris. I watched

Cassiopeia rise in the east. I watched the distant headlights of a car coming down the highway from Nipton flicker off and on as the road dipped and rose.

"He's coming," I whispered. My Bulova said it was twenty to midnight.

"Why are we whispering?" she whispered.

"We're whispering because we're frightened."

I stood up and surveyed three hundred and sixty degrees of desert very carefully through the night-vision goggles. Iron oxide in desert rocks glowed in the dark. As far as I could see, nothing moved—not a coyote in sight, not a bramble blown by the wind. Then, at 11:44 sharp on my dad's Bulova, one of those hundred-fifty-car Union Pacific freight trains hove into sight in the west. I took it for a rising planet until I saw the headlights on the first of the two locomotives and the penny dropped.

I must have cursed under my breath because Friday stirred. "What?"

"Forgot about the Union Pacific crawling past the hotel," I said. "That's how he's going to do it."

"Do what?"

Sure enough, only the abandoned hotel's second floor and roof were visible for the twelve minutes it took the train to pass. I studied the hotel's porch and ground floor through the goggles when I could see them again.

Nothing visible suggested life.

The headlights of the car coming from the direction of Nipton came over a rise. They looked a lot like the headlights of the Ferrari I'd seen in my rearview mirror when I was following Gava from in front. The car braked to a stop a football field down the road from Kelso Depot.

Friday flipped onto her stomach. "What's happening?"

"I'll give you my educated guess."

A man emerged from the car. I remembered Awlson's description of Gava: *The Wrestler was six foot even, one hundred seventy-five pounds, with good shoulders and a narrow waist. He held his head at an angle as if he was hard of hearing in one ear.*

The figure of the man coming down the highway matched the description Awlson had given me to a T—and looked a lot like the house dude on the high stool on the fourth floor of the Whistlestop gambling operation. I passed the goggles to Ornella. She adjusted them on her head. "It's him," she said flatly.

I asked her how she could be so sure.

She only repeated, "It's Emilio. I'd know him anywhere."

"Why do you keep calling him by his first name?"

I could feel her looking at me in the darkness. "That's what I called him when I posted the bail bond."

"Keep watching," I instructed her. I had a pretty good idea what she would see.

"Okay, he's climbed onto the hotel porch," she whispered. "He's looking around. He's studying the desert skyline—oh my God, he's looking directly at us. Do you think he can see us?"

"No. But he knows I'm out here somewhere."

"He's taken out a big envelope. He's waving it over his head at the desert. He's turned and gone into the hotel . . . I can see the faint beam of a flashlight inside flickering on the windows that still have panes. Ah, he's come back onto the porch. He's jumped off onto the sand path and starting up the road toward the car." I heard Ornella catch her breath. "It's not the same man, Lemuel. It's not Emilio. The man going back to the Ferrari is roughly the same height but he has a completely different way of walking. How can that be?"

"I figured Gava would still be in the hotel when I came to get the money," I said. "Didn't know how he'd pull it off. I was dumb not to think of the train. He had one of his cronies jump off the slow-moving Union Pacific when it passed Kelso Depot. It was the guy who jumped off the train who's going back to the car."

"Which means Emilio is waiting for you in the dark inside the hotel. He's surely armed. Oh my God, you can't go in there, Lemuel. Forget about taking him back for trial, forget about my losing the damned bail money." Friday sat up abruptly. "I don't want to lose you."

"I have the night-vision goggles," I reminded her. I took them from her and adjusted them on my head. The shadowy barefoot contessa crouching next to me on the tarpaulin materialized in her underwater bluish green majesty. For a moment I entertained the fantasy that I was sitting next to a mermaid. "I want you to make your way back to the Toyota in the wadi," I whispered. "I want you to wait for me there." When she didn't move, I said, "I'm asking you to do this."

"Why?"

"Why did you call him Emilio?"

I could see the mermaid look away. "What will you do?" she whispered.

"I'll make my way down to that pathway that runs from the hotel to the road. There are small dunes there. When I don't turn up in the hotel to retrieve the envelope, he'll get impatient—my guess is he'll give it an hour, two at the most. Then he'll come out on the porch in his stocking feet and look around. Then he'll sit on the edge of the porch, where the rail fell away, and put on his shoes. He'll figure I chickened out. He'll start up the pathway. That's when I'll take him. I'll have surprise on my side. I'll have the advantage of being able to see in the dark. He'll be blinder than a blind bat."

"You know how to do that kind of thing," she breathed. "You know how to deal with someone like . . . someone like Gava?"

"You were going to say Emilio."

"You didn't answer my question. You know how to take on Emilio?"

"I've been trained,"

"Who trained you?"

"Some very talented killers employed by the United States government."

She reached for my hand and pulled it under the fabric to her heart again. Her skin was cold to the touch, her heart racing, her body atremble. "I badly need to talk you out of this," she whispered.

That wasn't going to happen. The anger had risen in me

along with the adrenaline. Fact is I'd been startled the first time she called him Emilio, fact is I didn't appreciate her calling him Emilio all the time, fact is my imagination had filled in gaps in her story, fact is I supposed a lot of things. Fact is I was no longer weighed down by facts.

Fact is I was aching for a fight.

A fight is what I got.

I counted on him staying in the lobby for at least an hour, so I took the long way around, coming back up the pathway until I found a hidey-hole behind a small dune and a stump of a long-deceased tree. Gava held out in the dark of the lobby of the abandoned hotel for five hours and twelve minutes, according to the luminous dial on my father's Bulova. He was clearly a hoodlum with a lot of street savvy. He knew I was out here somewhere. He was waiting with a stalker's patience for me to come to him. I began to worry about that stalker's patience of his. I began to worry he'd wait until first light tinted the east, at which point my advantage—my ability to see in the dark—would be gone. When I finally spotted the shadow of a man standing on the porch of the hotel, I bottled up a sigh of relief for fear he might hear it. I carefully slipped the Bulova from my wrist and folded it into my handkerchief and buried it deep in my pocket.

Now I'll do the fight, or what I remember of it.

I have this memory of Gava coming along the pathway, all the while looking over his shoulder as if he couldn't believe I hadn't turned up; as if I might still turn up. Keeping my shoulder low, I slammed into him from his blind side (from the way he angled his head it may have been his deaf side, too). I heard the wind explode out of him along with a yowl of rage. I saw him sprawled on his back in the bluish green desert sand groping for the pistol in a shoulder holster when I kicked him hard in the groin and, dropping to my knees, brought my shoulder up into his chin. I thought I felt his jaw splinter under the impact. In my rage to draw blood, I am sorry to say I lost it—I lost whatever control I had on the caveman anger not far below the surface of all of us, I lost my dignity, I lost my memory of who I was trying to be since I'd stopped being who I was. I reared back and tried to hack the side of my hand down on the side of his neck but Gava was too young and too fast and too strong. Howling with pain, he rolled away from me and brought a knee up into my thigh and managed a karate chop to my upper left arm that sent a current of pain shooting down to my wrist, leaving it numb. He was scrambling to his knees breathing hard and prying his pistol out of its holster when I heel-stomped him in the back of one of his knees and kicked the pistol out into the desert and backed off to one side in the hope of socking him when he came off the ground. But he never came off the ground—he rolled and came up in a crouch groping for something taped to his ankle, which is when I remembered the sweet little two-shot derringer. I saw it in his fist but I have no memory of hearing it go off. He must have pulled the trigger because I felt the wasp-sting of the bullet grazing my neck—and I had this crazy thought, now I had another wound for Friday to lick. Before Gava could get off a second shot, I hit him with one of the combat moves I'd learned the hard way—I'd been on the receiving end of it in the back alley of a souk in Peshawar. I plunged in low and hard, crunching into his rib cage with my head. The brittle sound of ribs cracking reverberated through the bluish green emptiness of the night. With my arm that still had feeling below the wrist I bunched my fingers into a fist and swung up where I thought his jaw ought to be, and nearly broke my wrist when my knuckles connected with something rock hard. I heard Gava trying to vomit. With the wind and the fight knocked out of him he melted into the desert floor, groaning in agony. I kicked him hard in his good ear to be sure he wasn't faking.

He was not faking.

I have a dim memory of looking for his pistol and not finding it, of retrieving the derringer from the pathway, of tying Gava's feet in a makeshift sling using the sleeves of my khaki jacket and dragging him back down the pathway, feet first, to the hotel. I wrestled him onto the porch and into the hotel and propped him against what had once been the check-in counter, then secured his wrists behind his back with a coil of telephone wire I'd spotted under the staircase. I folded back his legs and lashed his ankles to his wrists for good measure, put the night-vision goggles and the derringer on the check-in counter and went outside to the barrel filled with rainwater and splashed some on my face and wasp-wound. Then I soaked both my hands in the barrel up to the elbows for a long moment. When I pulled my hands free I noticed the fourth finger of my right hand hanging limply from its joint—the tendon had been busted when I slugged Gava in the jaw. I jury-rigged a splint with a sliver of wood from the porch railing and wrapped my handkerchief around the splint and the finger and splashed more water on my face and neck. I felt a certain after-shock calmness returning. My breathing wasn't normal but it was going in the right direction. I shook myself the way a dog does when it comes in from the rain. First light was starting to smudge the horizon in the east when I heard a muffled cry of terror and then the sound of gagging coming from the lobby. I went inside to discover Ornella Neppi kneeling over the Wrestler, her skirt whipped back, her bare knees clamped against his ears, the derringer clutched in her small fist and jammed into Gava's mouth. With her free hand she pulled a blonde wig from that silver astronaut knapsack of hers and set it askew on her head.

And to my everlasting regret the missing pieces of the awful puzzle fell into place.

Friday was the blonde bombshell girlfriend that Gava took back to his condo and beat up while he was making love to her.

"Now do you recognize me?" Ornella asked Gava in an ugly whisper.

Gagging on the barrel of the derringer in his mouth, he managed a terrorized nod.

I found my voice. "Don't do that," I called softly.

"He hurt me," Friday sobbed. "He hurt me so much there is no me, there's only the hurt."

"I've seen the welts—I never swallowed the story of a car accident." I took a step in her direction. "Killing him won't solve your problem," I said.

She never so much as glanced at me. "Killing him will make him vanish from my dreams," she said in a dead voice. "Killing him will make me better." And she angled the barrel so that it was pointing toward the endless expanse of universe over our heads and she pulled the trigger. Gava's skull exploded, splattering brain matter on everything within a fifteen-meter stain radius.

I thought I'd seen it all but here was something I hadn't seen—me sinking back on my haunches wiping someone's brains off my face with my sleeve, me suddenly suffocating under the dead weight of the endless expanse of universe over my head, me trying to remember who I'd been after I'd escaped from my first stain radius back in the Hindu Kush Mountains.

Twenty-seven

You didn't have to be Philip Marlowe to understand I was in a jam. With a corpse instead of a prisoner on my hands, the situation was delicate, to say the least. I could almost hear the prosecutor summing up to the jury:

Fact: Ornella Neppi engaged the accused, Lemuel Gunn, a former CIA agent who was expelled from the Agency for reasons too secret to spell out in open court, an occasional private detective working out of a mobile home in Hatch, New Mexico, a reject from society, to track down Emilio Gava so she wouldn't be out the $125,000 she posted as bond.
Fact: Somewhere along the way this same Lemuel Gunn became Ornella Neppi's lover.
Fact: He noticed the welts on her rib cage and discovered that Emilio Gava had brutalized her during a six-month liaison.
Fact: In a jealous rage, he lured Gava to an abandoned hotel, overpowered him, breaking several of his ribs and his jaw in the process, and then cold-bloodedly

jammed a derringer into the mouth of the bound vic-
tim and fired a bullet into his brain.
Ladies and gentlemen of the jury, this is commonly
called first-degree homicide.

I don't know how much time passed before Friday joined
me on the hotel porch. I was sitting with my back to the wall
squinting into the sun rising over the Kelso dunes. Without
a word, she settled down next to me, her shoulder touching
mine. "I didn't intend to—"

"You should have stayed in the Toyota like I—"

"I heard a shot, I thought he might have killed you—"

We were talking past each other, not to each other.

"We need to notify the authorities—"

"—wrap the body in the tarpaulin and bury it in the
desert. Nobody will be the wiser—"

I shook my head. "Listen up, Friday, we have to take our
chances with the police."

She turned on me and I couldn't miss noticing that her
face and hair were speckled with Gava's brains and blood.
"Can't you see, Lemuel, I won't *have* a chance. If I'd killed
him when he was abusing me, a jury would have been sym-
pathetic. But this will look like premeditated murder. Look,
there never was a girlfriend named Jennifer Leffler with a
deed to a condo. I was the girlfriend. I put up bail without
collateral because he was my lover, because he swore he would
beat the charge and we would go away together. When I
realized he was going to jump bail and run out on both the
$125,000 bond and me, something in me snapped. When I

asked you to find him, I didn't give a damn about the $125,000. I wanted you to find him so the Corsican in me could kill him."

"You need to tell your story to a judge," I said softly. I found myself talking to her the way you talk to a child coming off a tantrum. "I'll find you a good lawyer. You need to show the jury the welts. You need to convince them—"

"You told me you were eager to share my pain," Friday said. She pulled her dress off one shoulder, exposing the ugly welts on her rib cage. "You be the judge and jury, Lemuel. You try the case. If you find me guilty, I swear to you we'll call the police. If you find me innocent—if you decide it was justifiable homicide—we'll bury the body and get on with our lives."

Thinking it would calm her if I heard her out, thinking we could still call the police when she'd finished, I accepted the challenge. On the porch of the abandoned Kelso hotel, with the rising sun burning the chill off the desert, I listened.

Shrugging her shoulder back into the dress, she noticed the nick in my neck. She spit on the hem of her dress and used the moistened fabric to wipe the blood from my wound. "I met Emilio Gava one night at a block party in Albuquerque," she said, her voice hauntingly soft, her eyes tightly shut as if keeping them shut would stem a tide of tears. "He was lean and good-looking and a smooth talker and a good listener. I'd never known anyone like him before. He was uneducated and coarse and rough but he didn't play intellectual games, he didn't beat around the bush, he came right out and told me he wanted to have sex with me. So you said it yourself, Lemuel. You said we are different lovers with different people. You said it was completely mysterious and completely magical—how one person can transform you into an eager and ardent lover and another can barely get you to perform adequately. Was it my fault if Emilio transformed me into an eager and ardent lover? To put it crudely, he turned me on. At first the lovemaking was gentle, but gradually he began to explore the violent side of the sex act."

The violent side of the sex act! I almost choked on the words. I muttered, "Lady, we're not talking about the same act."

"Oh, yes we are, dearest Lemuel. You really were born into the wrong century. You're out of sync with this one. You see it from a man's point of view—you see sex as a coupling, like two cars in a train attaching themselves to each other with a gentle crunch. Women see it as a penetration, an invasion, an assault with or without battery, which leaves scars, some of which are visible, most of which are concealed. Can't you understand, Lemuel? At different points in our lives we are different people. These points can be days apart, even hours, it doesn't matter. Women love differently than men. We spend our lives trying to figure out what it means to be female. For the six months that we were together, Emilio imposed his definition on me. To the Emilios of this world, to be female is to be at the service of men, the receptacle in which they deposit their seed when they get the urge."

Pushing herself to her feet, Ornella went to the barrel of rainwater and, wetting the hem of her skirt, began to wipe the blood off of her face and arms and chest and hair. After a while she walked over to what was left of the porch railing and stared out into the waves of heat beginning to rise off the desert floor. I realized she was still talking so I got up to stand next to her. She was saying something about having been a battered child. She was describing what it was like to have lived a lifetime of pain. The words and phrases emerged in a single tone of voice, as if dredging up the past had numbed her vocal cords. "Every time my father beat me I took it for granted that I'd done something wrong," she was saying. "I couldn't figure out what but I took it for granted I deserved the beating. The punishment made me feel as if I had expiated the sin, whatever it was, that I was Daddy's little girl again. Oh, how he would cuddle me and fondle me after each beating. Over time the pain of the beating was transformed into pleasure, and the line between the two blurred. I became addicted to this pain-pleasure syndrome. Emilio picked up where my father, long since dead, left off; the brutal sex with Emilio was a continuation of this pattern." She turned to look at me. I could have sworn the seaweed green in her eyes had faded to what I took to be mourning gray. Blinking back unshed tears, she said, "He beat me and fucked me and cuddled me. And the addict I was then kept coming back for more."

When she finally ran out of words, I wandered off into the desert to sort through my emotions. A tepid breeze stirred paper cups and cellophane wrappers that had been tossed from passing cars over the years. Overhead, two kingfishers, with the distinctive white collar around their necks, circled looking for lizards. I watched them for a long time. I watched the slowly bloating contrails of a jet heading in the direction of the Pacific. The sound of the jet engines reached my ears well after the plane had passed, which meant it was flying faster than the speed of sound; which meant the sound, racing after the plane, would catch up with it on a Los Angeles runway. There is something about flying faster than the sound your engines produce, something about the infinity of space that birds and planes inhabit, that reduces life and love and homicide to puny details in the history of the universe. Gunn, the philosopher king spouting his half-baked theory of relativity. I remembered the first time I'd set eyes on Friday, with her nipple pointing straight at me through the flimsy fabric of her dress. She'd looked as if she were hanging on by her fingertips but I couldn't figure out to what. Now I knew. She was hanging on to sanity. She'd been mauled, physically and mentally. The instinct that pushed her to kill Emilio was as old as the human race, as old as the first man who mastered walking on his hind legs so that he could use the front ones to grip a club. If you're mauled, you maul back.

Add to this the fact that Emilio Gava a.k.a. Silvio Restivo, the Wrestler with a penchant for brutal sex, had blood on his hands; he had set up Salvatore Baldini for the sniper. Add to this the fact that the Delta-Foxtrot people who had murdered three females and blown out the brains of the especially tall mujahid on the Hindu Kush had never been charged with a crime.

Back at the porch I found Ornella where I'd left her, staring from the half-broken railing into the desert. "What have you decided?" she whispered.

"I've decided killing Gava was justifiable homicide. I've decided no jury would find you guilty of killing a killer. I've decided to bury his body in the dunes. I've decided we need to quit this stain radius in the hope that we can get on with our lives and our loves."

She opened her eyes and the tears spilled from them. "Lemuel, Lemuel," she sobbed as she came into my arms.

The rest was a matter of work in the final inch. I retrieved a length of white plastic stashed under the staircase and folded Gava's corpse into it. I brought the Toyota down from the wadi and, with Friday's help, loaded the body into the back of the car. I found Gava's handgun in the sand off the pathway. I wiped the prints off it and off the derringer and buried both in a rabbit hole on the side of a dune a good mile into the Mojave. Then I drove deep into a tangle of wadis and, using the folding army shovel, dug a grave in the sand. I dragged the plastic into the hole and covered it with sand and big flat stones. I figured the wadi would be filled with water after the summer rains. With any luck the body would never be found—Gava would just be a hoodlum who had gone missing from the witness protection program; gone missing from the face of the earth.

Ornella, meanwhile, had soaked her dress in the barrel

of rainwater and used it to wipe most of the stains off the
walls and the check-in counter. To the naked eye the lobby
of the Kelso Depot hotel looked long abandoned. It would
have taken a forensic expert to identify the smudges on the
walls as human blood. Friday had rinsed her dress and put
it on sopping wet and was standing in the sun trying to dry
it when I came back from the wadis. We caught our respective breaths, I took a last look around. Friday smiled a thin
smile. "Thank you for being here, Lemuel," she said. "Thank
you for being." I wasn't sure how you said thank you for a
thank you so I just nodded. We climbed into the Toyota
and headed back toward Nipton to collect my belongings.

Which is when I discovered the note pinned to the door
of the Clara Bow room. I somehow knew it spelled trouble.

Trouble it was. *Call this number urgently,* somebody had
scrawled on the back of an envelope. I recognized the phone
number—it was France-Marie's, my French Canadian accountant in Las Cruces.

I used the pay phone in the general store. France-Marie
came on the line. "Kubra called," she said. "She sounded
kind of funny. She said you should call her at a Nevada number. What's she doing in Nevada, Lemuel? I thought she
was supposed to be at her junior college in California. I asked
her if it could wait until you got back to Hatch. She said no.
She said it couldn't wait. The way she said it made it sound
almost like she needed help, and quick."

I dialed the number in Nevada. A man answered. "That
you, Gunn? You took your sweet time calling. Here, wait a
sec—"

Kubra came on the line. "It's me, Gunn."

"You okay, Kubra?"

"Not really."

"What's wrong, little lady?"

"Plenty's wrong," she said. I could hear the strain in her voice, as if she were fighting off a persuasive terror. "I thought you'd sent them to get me, that's what they said when—" She didn't finish the sentence. I heard her cry out in pain.

A man comes on the line. "Listen up, dickhead," he growled, "you are holding one of ours, we are holding one of yours. Like we suppose you will be interested in an exchange."

Ornella was at my elbow. "Who is it?" she whispered.

I snarled into the phone, "If anything happens to my kid—" I took a deep breath. "Okay, sure, let's trade," My thoughts were racing ahead of the words forming on my lips. "There's a small-sized problem. We had a fight. Your man can't walk so well."

The gravel voice actually laughed. "No sweat. We'll accept delivery in a wheelchair."

I told him I'd scout around for a suitable site and would phone back at four that afternoon.

"Four, okay. Don't talk to the fuzz. You talk to the fuzz, you never see the girl no more." The line went dead in my ear.

I suppose the blood must have drained from my face because Friday looked frightened. "It's your doing," I burst out. "If you hadn't—"

The lovely lady who tended to the counter and her two

customers were all staring at me. I took Ornella by the elbow and steered her out of the store. Standing at the edge of the Mojave, I explained the situation to her in a few brittle words. She looked at me, heartbroken. "Oh my God!" she whispered.

"I've got to figure something out," I said.

I turned and walked across the tracks into the desert. Ornella trailed after me several paces behind. I was in the mood for an orgy of recriminations. "If my daughter winds up dead because of you—"

I heard her words over my sore shoulder, the one I'd used to break Gava's jaw. "What will you do? Could you bring yourself to kill me, Lemuel? Maybe you don't have the stomach for that. Maybe you'll only beat me up like Emilio did, with short little punches to the breasts that make me gasp for breath."

I winced when she called him Emilio again. I was afraid to turn and face her, afraid that I would punch her in the chest. Violence begets violence. I kept walking, walking and thinking. Behind me, Friday had the good sense to shut up. Slowly the bits and pieces of a plan began to fall into place. It started with the wheelchair and went on from there. It was a long shot but my only shot. We were deep into the desert when I finally turned around. Ornella sank to her knees, her face speckled with grains of fine sand that had stuck to her skin where it was streaked with tears. "I would go back and change things if I could," she murmured.

"Here's what we'll do," I said.

Twenty-eight

We were crouching next to the Toyota on the rise in the desert across the tracks and up from Kelso Depot, not far from where we'd set out the tarpaulin and watched Gava's Ferrari come down the road the night before. Gava's body, which I'd excavated from his wadi grave and brushed pretty much clean of sand, was propped up with a neck brace and lashed onto the motorized wheelchair in front of the car. I'd rented both the brace and the wheelchair from the medical supplies store above the Beauty Emporium in Searchlight. The idea had come to me when I remembered Mr. Baldini tooling around his office in a motorized wheelchair. Max-Leo, the son in Millman & Son Hard and Soft Ware, had jury-rigged a remote joystick from one of his remote-controlled model planes so I could steer the wheelchair from a distance. Max-Leo was a whiz kid with electronics. He'd produced a two-deck tape player and toggled back and forth between my tape of Gava calling the police and a virgin cassette, recording from one tape to the other, until I had Gava saying what I wanted. Then Max-Leo had wired on a battery-powered loudspeaker so that I could broadcast

Gava's voice into the desert. Friday, meanwhile, had rummaged around the shelves of Searchlight's secondhand apparel boutique and come away with black tights, black Reeboks, long black opera gloves and a long-sleeved midnight blue turtleneck sweater. She'd blackened her face with a cosmetic she kept in her astronaut knapsack for when she worked life-sized puppets with sticks. I'd caught her act in that Pueblo youth club, I was about to catch it again. Crouching next to me in the darkness, you'd never know she was there if you didn't know she was there. I'd dialed an 800 number from a booth in Searchlight to double-check the Union Pacific freight train schedule, then phoned the Nevada number again to set a time and a place for the exchange— eleven thirty on the nose at Kelso Depot. God willing, my live Kubra for their dead Gava. I'd used the last of the daylight to scout the desert trails around Kelso before going to ground. Or should I say going to sand.

I could see Ornella was jumpy. I needed her to perform flawlessly, so I tried to calm her down. "This is going to work out," I said.

Friday said, "I'll never forgive myself if it doesn't. If only—"

The wind had come up and with it the sand. Both of us were rubbing it out of our eyes. When the Ruggeri crowd showed up they would, thank God, be rubbing it out of their eyes, too. "We have to deal with the situation we have," I said. "There's no place for ifs."

"*If* is the storyline of my life."

"Not mine."

"You've been lucky."

"I like to think I made my luck."

Headlights flickered down the road, then a second pair, then a third. Three cars appeared over a rise on the tarmac. Two of the cars pulled up behind the hotel, the third car, a long black limousine, parked alongside the hotel's dilapidated porch. Its headlights dimmed and then went off. I could hear car doors opening. Watching through the night-vision goggles, I could make out four men emerging into the bluish green seascape from the limousine. Men from the other cars joined them—I counted nine men standing on either side of the limousine. Several cradled rifles in the crook of their arms. One of the men had both his hands up to his face. I supposed he was looking through night-vision binoculars.

The headlights of the limousine blinked on and off twice. I reached through the open window of the Toyota and flashed my headlights twice in reply.

A handheld spotlight swept the desert and came to rest on Gava, strapped into the wheelchair.

From the hotel porch, the hoarse voice of an older man called through a tinny megaphone, "You okay, Silvio?"

Ornella, squatting behind the wheelchair, worked the sticks that we had attached to the backs of the wrists of the very dead Emilio Gava. Seen from the limousine, seen by the Ruggeri foot soldiers with sand in their eyes, Gava must have looked as if he were waving his arms over his head as his voice, broadcast from a speaker Max-Leo had wired to the tape deck, echoed over the dunes.

"I'm awright, I'm awright, take my woid for it, huh?"

From the hotel porch, the hoarse voice started to ask a question but Gava's voice cut him off. *"Awright, I have not got all night. What do you say we put this show on the road, huh?"*

The thin figure of a young woman appeared in front of the limousine. A man reached behind her to untie her hands. Massaging her wrists, she looked back at the older man on the porch, then started walking toward the tracks and the desert. At the Toyota, I turned on the wheelchair's motor from my remote and then worked the joystick so that it started slowly down the track toward the railroad crossing. The handheld spotlight followed it. I took a quick look at my Bulova—it was 11:44. I caught the distant whimper of the Union Pacific freight train as its headlights appeared around a bend of the tracks. The wheelchair and Kubra crossed each other at the tracks. Kubra slowed to take a look at the man—oh, was I proud of her then. She must have noticed that his head was propped up in a neck brace, she couldn't have missed the dried bloodstains on his skin and shirt, it surely dawned on her that the man was stone dead. She must have seen the note I'd pinned to the chest of the corpse because she looked uphill in my direction, then back at the Ruggeri crew around the limousine. I could see from her body language that she'd pretty much figured out what had happened. "Thanks a lot and the same to you, you son of a bitch," she shouted at the man in the wheelchair—loud enough for the goons back at the limousine to think the two had exchanged pleasantries. "Resist the impulse to run," I said under my breath—and by golly, Kubra did. She kept walking on up the track, closing the distance between her and the Toyota with each lovely step.

"Your daughter's got a lot of gumption," Ornella said in my ear.

"What she has is lot of guts. That's how she survived Afghanistan."

Two figures detached themselves from the others at the limousine. I could have sworn one of them was that Mario character who had scratched his diamond ring across the fender of my Studebaker. I recognized him because he was on the short side, short and thickset, with a fedora planted on his head. He walked up to the tracks to meet the man in the wheelchair. Under my breath, I muttered, "Come on, Kubra, run for it now." Then I called out, "Run, Kubra," and she did, she ran with the long-legged strides of a beautiful girl who had run for her life before. To me it looked as if her feet barely touched the ground.

Across the tracks, the bellow of rage from Mario as he reached the wheelchair was drowned out by the shrill whistle of the Union Pacific locomotive coming down the tracks. The goons at the limousine produced pistols, the men with rifles snapped the butts to their shoulders, but before any of them could get off a shot the locomotive hauling freight across Arizona was on the tracks between them and us.

It was one of those endless trains and it gave me the precious minutes I needed to bundle Kubra and Friday into the four-wheel-drive Toyota and plunge back into the Mojave along the trails I'd scouted that afternoon.

"Why'd you kill him, Gunn?" Kubra asked once we'd put some distance between us and Kelso Depot.

"It was me who killed him," Friday announced.

I pulled off the night-vision goggles and flicked on the Toyota's high beams. By happenstance we were passing through the wadi where I'd buried Gava, and then deburied him. "It was justifiable homicide," I explained.

"Who is she?" Kubra looked sharply at Ornella. "Who are you?" she demanded.

"My name's Ornella. Ornella Neppi. Your father calls me Friday, which was the day of the week our life lines first crossed." Ornella touched my elbow. "I've become very attached to the nickname."

I could see Kubra's head in the rearview mirror. She reached for my shoulder. I was so elated to have her in the car I didn't tell her it was sore. "I have a lot of catching up to do," she said. "Who was the dead guy, Gunn?"

"A thug."

"What did you write on the note you pinned to his chest?"

"I wrote *An eye for an eye.* I signed it Giancarlo Baldini."

"Who is Giancarlo Baldini?" Kubra asked.

"He's the godfather of the Baldini family—his son was set up for a kill by the dead goon in the wheelchair."

"That's going to provoke gang war between the two casino families," Friday guessed.

"Couldn't happen to nicer mobsters," I said.

Twenty-nine

To my eternal relief, Giancarlo Baldini didn't deposit a not-so-small packet of money in an out-of-the-way bank by way of bounty for eliminating the Ruggeri soldier who had set up the hit on his son Salvatore. It wasn't hard to figure out why. In the settling of scores at Clinch Corners that followed my malevolent *An eye for an eye* note pinned to the corpse at Kelso Depot, Giancarlo, the don of the Baldini family, met his maker when the elevator in his casino lost its brakes and plunged from his office to the casino's subbasement, the one where they stored broken slot machines. I think those two proctologists assigned to the elevator were killed with him.

And that was just the beginning.

In the days that followed, stories of a Mafia feud in Clinch Corners, Nevada, made headlines in the *Albuquerque Times Herald*. Two rival Mafia families, which ran casinos across the highway from each other, were at war. There had been seven murders. One of the casinos and a members-only joint on the Colorado River code-named Whistlestop had been burned to the ground. Bombs had exploded in several mobile homes and automobiles. State police had moved in and arrested eighteen members of the two families, some on murder charges, others on income tax evasion and racketeering charges.

The FBI's regional witness protection guru, Charlie Coffin, has since become a good pal of mine. He slipped Kubra into the FBI program—he outfitted her with one of those pint-sized mobile telephones so I could check in with her from time to time and gave her a new identity in case a stray Baldini or Ruggeri got it into his head to get back at me through my daughter for Gava and the subsequent end of the Clinch Corners armistice. Charlie was glad to help out, the more so since I had no intention of going to the newspapers with the story of how the FBI fell for Emilio Gava's story, which led to the sniper assassination of a member of a rival Mafia family already in the federal witness protection program. We were drinking beer in a roadside bar and keeping track, from afar, of the dustup at Clinch Corners when Charlie pointed out that there were still some loose ends to tie up.

"How," he asked, scratching his balding head in puzzlement, "did the Ruggeris discover that a private investigator named Lemuel Gunn was on the trail of one of their soldiers, Emilio Gava?"

"Excellent question," I said. On a paper napkin, I drew up a list of possibilities: There was Lyle Leggett, the *Las Cruces Star* photographer; Detective Awlson of the Las Cruces police; D.D. Dillinger, the bartender at the Blue Grass who dreams of inventing a new cocktail and giving his name to it; Alvin Epley, the concierge at East of Eden Gar-

dens; Jesus Oropesa, the Chicano drug dealer; R. Russell
Fontenrose, the three-hundred-dollar-an-hour fancy-pants
attorney; the East of Eden regulars in Emilio's Sunday night
poker shootout, Frank Uzzel, Hank and Millie Kugler, and
Hattie Hillslip. All of the above knew I was walking back
the cat on Gava. Somewhere along the way one of these
people alerted the Ruggeris, who then nosed around Hatch,
found out about Kubra and kidnapped her. Through a process of elimination, based mostly on instinct and my reading of character, I ruled out one candidate after another
until I was finally left with three: Jesus Oropesa, R. Russell
Fontenrose and Hattie Hillslip, who just might have had a
secret affair with Emilio Gava.

"Leave me take care of this for you," Charlie said.

Later that afternoon he turned up at the Once in a Blue
Moon with a smug grin on his face. He explained that he
had gotten the Chicano drug pusher's phone number from
Detective Awlson and looked up the other two in the phone
book. Slipping a growl into his already gravelly voice, he'd
phoned each of the three candidates.

I was hanging on Charlie's every word.

"The Chicano kid told me to fuck off. Hattie Hillslip
thought I was the director of the Las Cruces old-age home
calling to thank her for her volunteer work."

"What about R. Russell?"

"Ah, R. Russell. I had one hell of a time getting past the
secretary of his secretary. Finally, pretending to be affiliated
with the President's Council of Economic Advisers, I was
put through to the man himself. 'I'm calling to thank you

for services rendered,'" I told him. 'We got long memories. We don't forget favors like the one you did us.'

"And?"

"R. Russell cleared his throat, then mumbled, 'This is not something we should be talking about on the phone.'" He must have had a sudden twinge of doubt, because he blurted out, 'Hold on, who is this?'"

I'd brought in two cold bottles of Mexican Modelos and was kneading the bottletop from one of them into a ball with my fingers. "How the hell do you do that?" Charlie asked.

I smiled. "I don't do it. Pent-up anger does it. What'd you say to R. Russell?"

"I told him my name wasn't important. I told him I was an amigo of Lemuel Gunn, a private detective who had once admired his antique globes. I told him the aforementioned Mr. Gunn happened to be sitting next to me listening to the conversation. I told him Mr. Gunn was smiling a particularly nasty smile—if I didn't know Mr. Gunn was incapable of violence, I would have described it as a brutal smile that hinted at cruel and unusual punishment. I told him I suspected he would be hearing directly from Mr. Gunn when he least expected it. It could be in a week or a month or a year. I told him to stay tuned."

"R. Russell's going to have a lot of sleepless nights," I said. "Thanks, sport."

"Hey, my pleasure," Coffin said.

Thirty

I drove the Studebaker over to Las Cruces and picked up
some army survey maps of Arizona east of the Grand Canyon, the area known as the Painted Desert. I bought a
dozen six-packs of Dos Equis, a two-week supply of food
staples, and filled four twenty-gallon jerry cans with gasoline. Back at the Once in a Blue Moon, I checked to make
sure the spare batteries were charged, and phoned the state
weather office in Gallup and got the recorded voice that
gives you the long-range forecast for the desert. Then I rented
a four-wheel-drive pickup from the guy who owns the mobile home park in Hatch. As the sun was dipping behind
the pines, I hitched the Once in a Blue Moon up to it. Friday pulled herself up into the pickup's copilot seat. She was
wearing a pair of white jogging shorts with slits up the sides
and a white halter that revealed almost as much as it concealed. I had to admit she was a very attractive package, welts
and all.

"So with all that food and beer, you'd think we were
heading off to Australia or something," she remarked. "Are
you sure there's nothing I can do to help?"

"You're helping by being here," I said. I slid behind the pickup's wheel, started the motor, and pulled Once in a Blue Moon out of its berth and onto Interstate 25, heading north for Gallup and the Painted Desert.

I've always liked to drive at night—the roads empty out, which makes towing Mr. Douglas Fairbanks Jr.'s enormous mobile home a piece of cake. We were both lost in our thoughts for a long while. "Hot night," Friday murmured at one point. Out of the corner of my eye I saw her dip both hands behind her back in that lovely gesture females have perfected, and her halter fell away.

In the darkness we exchanged smiles. We'd come a long way from the weightless kiss she'd deposited on my lips in the parking lot of the slow-food restaurant.

With my bare-breasted contessa sitting next to me, I worked my way north and, skirting Albuquerque at Los Lunas, headed west. By sunup the next morning we had put Gallup behind us and could make out the shimmering heat rising off the floor of the desert. I had spent three weeks in the Painted Desert once, muddling through a CIA survival course. Some British sergeants who had cut their teeth on the Sahara taught us how to spot topographical features that indicated there was fresh water under the ground; taught us how to trap and eat lizards, which was not something I really wanted to learn. Using the army maps and the hour hand of my wristwatch to determine due south, I came across the old single-lane road that meandered through the eroded layers of colored clay and came to a dead end at a spot where the Little Colorado River widened into something resembling a lake.

The days that followed passed in a kind of pipe-dream mist, the component parts of which were one part sun to one part sensuality. We got up with the sun and went to sleep with the sun. In between we explored the riverbank for hours in either direction. We swam whenever our skins felt warm to the touch. We touched all the time. I came to cherish the lovemaking after the swimming, with her glistening cool body leaning over me to shade me. Gradually the welts on her rib cage faded, the way a bad dream fades in the brilliant light of the morning. Most of the time we wore shorts and nothing else. I rigged a laundry line from a dead tree to the Once in a Blue Moon, but there never seemed to be anything to hang on it. I taught Ornella to open her eyes underwater—she saw swarms of minnows and beautifully colored rocks. She taught me to open my eyes above water—I saw the Little Colorado tickling the sand out from under the soles of my feet as we prowled the riverbank, and the tiny insects scurrying into the holes the water punched in Friday's footprints.

We didn't talk all that much. Most of the communication between us took place in the spaces between the words, in the lingering soft silences after lovemaking. She told me she had fallen in love with me and repeated it at the most unlikely moments, as if it was a hidden treasure she had stumbled across. I told her that I was falling in love with her. I didn't tell her that I didn't like her—I didn't have the courage, and I didn't want to break the spell. Both of us understood that we were inventing ourselves as we went along. The self I invented, the person I made an effort to be when I wasn't being me, tried hard not to believe that love and murder were at opposite ends of the spectrum; tried hard not to think that one sucked energy and life from the other. I never put this into so many words but I didn't have to. She picked up on it from the way I had of closing my eyes and keeping them closed for several seconds and breathing hard through my nose. She picked up on it from the lovemaking. The acts of sex, the orgasms, were the same, but that became the problem—they should have been like the groundswells of an ocean that grew deeper and longer as you approached a coast.

In a sense, knowing where we were going—we were going nowhere—freed us. Every touch, every glance was heavy with nostalgia for what might have been. If only. If. Ifs lined up as far as the eye could see. An army of ifs saluting every time we walked the riverbank, our hips touching, to watch from a spit of sand as the sunset reverberated across the clay-colored desert.

So we drifted, and then we drifted apart.

Friday was the first to put it into words. "If I'd known the choice was between loving you or killing him," she said one night as we watched the sun sizzle into the horizon, "I would have . . ."

She turned to look at me. An infinitely sad smile disfigured her seaweed green eyes. She was too honest to lie. "Damn it, Lemuel, I would have killed him anyhow." She took my hand and held the back of it to her breast. "I told you I'd moved on from where I couldn't hurt a fly."

"I guess I know that. I guess that's the heart of the problem. In a funny way I suppose I'm jealous of Emilio Gava—your unfinished business with him was more important than your unfinished business with me."

I tried not to think about it, tried not to logic it out, but I could no more control the lobe of my brain that agonized over these things than I could control my pleasure at watching her wade naked in the river in search of colored rocks. I had liked a lot of women in my time, but some twitch of the brain had kept me from loving them, or at least loving them enough to abandon everything for them. Now Gunn, the eternal drifter, had finally come across someone he could love, but he didn't much like her.

I came at what that tough old king of Siam would have called the puzzlement from every point of the compass, but I somehow couldn't get a handle on it. I couldn't bring myself to like the part of her that was able to jam a pistol into the mouth of a bound man and see the terror in the back of his eyes and take pleasure from it and pull the trigger, no matter how justified the homicide.

It crossed my mind that I was using this as an excuse not to stay involved. Still, I couldn't shake off the doubt that was growing in me like a tumor. As a woman, as a lover, Friday was more than I'd bargained for, more than I'd ever experienced. As a human being, she was less.

"So you're a nasty piece of work, Gunn," she announced out of the blue one evening after we'd made love.

"Why am I a nasty piece of work?"

"I'm trying, you're not."

I educated her, which is what you do with people you love. "It's got to come without trying, my beautiful bruised lady of the lake. You can't fake the emotions you think you ought to have."

"You told me you loved me. I was lost in the desert—I wanted to be lost with you."

"I do love you."

"So what's the matter?" When I didn't answer, she shuddered. "You can't get it out of your head, can you?"

I shook my head no.

"You're like all the others—what you really hate is that I had sex with him."

She still didn't understand. "At my age," I said, "you don't date many virgins."

What had to happen happened. One dazzling morning I backed the pickup up to the mobile home and hitched the two together and we headed back down the one-lane road toward civilization. From time to time I caught a glimpse of Friday, shirtless in the seat next to me, her right arm dangling lazily out the window, her head angled away from the sun, her breasts glistening with perspiration, staring at a horizon beyond the one I could see.

At one halt to fill the gas tank from the jerry cans, she disappeared into the Once in a Blue Moon for a moment. Later, when we were on the road again, she came up with the things we'd exchanged back in Nipton—the war-wound hunk of shrapnel I'd worn on my key chain, her St. Christopher medallion, tokens of an eternal love with a shorter half-life than we'd counted on. She even produced the beer cap compressed into a ball, a souvenir of the power of anger. She pulled the shoelace from one of her sneakers and strung the mementos together.

"So you're getting off on being superior to me," she said with sudden bitterness. "I hate that. I hate the part of you I don't love."

The desert, streaked with shimmering seams of yellow and red clay, seemed for an instant like the surface of a planet that wouldn't sustain human life. With a tight-lipped smile playing on her Scott Fitzgerald lips, Friday tossed the tokens out the window. I thought vaguely of fixing my position and marking it on my army map and calling it in to the survey people so they could warn lovers to avoid this particular patch of quicksand.

It was dark by the time we made the outskirts of Albuquerque. I pulled into a trailer park for the night and whipped up some pasta al dente with tomato sauce and opened a Bordeaux that'd been bottled at a château, so the label informed us. We managed to kill that bottle and half of a second one and made believe we were more drunk than we were so we wouldn't have to face the awkwardness of a last lovemaking. In the morning I heard water running in the shower and remembered the times I had squeezed in with her to lather down that long-stemmed body of hers, and I thought maybe I was making the mistake of my life, and then I thought I should give up thinking inasmuch as it is clearly dangerous for your mental health.

After a quick breakfast, I uncoupled the Once in a Blue Moon and drove Friday in the pickup to the Albuquerque airport and stood like a dumb waiter, shifting my weight from one foot to the other, while she bought a one-way ticket to a world away. I muttered something about the weather being too overcast to fly. I muttered something about the plane having to defy the pull of gravity to get off the ground. I muttered something about this being the thirteenth day of the month.

She caught her breath. "It's really not complicated," she whispered. "All you have to do is pipe-dream me into not going."

When I couldn't bring myself to say anything, she smiled one of those barefoot contessa smiles of hers. The traces of joy that had seeped into it in the last weeks were gone. "Fuck you," she said.

"Fuck me," I agreed.

I kissed her good-bye in front of the metal detector and waved and nodded and waved again when she reached the other side. Then I picked up my mobile home and crawled back to Hatch like a dog with his tail tucked between his legs, sick to the gut knowing my best years were behind me. The late-night music on the car radio was a golden oldie—one of Kubra's favorites from Billy Joel's *An Innocent Man,* which reminded me of what I wasn't. I lost track of time, I lost track of place. Savoring every heartache, I concentrated on the white ribbon that runs down the middle of the road hoping against hope it would lead me somewhere I hadn't been.

That night I arranged some cushions on the roof of the Once in a Blue Moon and stretched out on them to see if I could hear what Kubra calls the music of the spheres originating in the endless expanse of universe over our heads.

All I heard was the empty awful silence of my life.

Gunn, you prick, what have you done?